"Finish me!" the injured gunman pleaded. "Oh, God! For the love of Christ, finish me!"

"You would have left me to die in agony if things had turned out differently. You'd have stood by and laughed as I died. There'd be no merciful bullet from you if I was in your place right now," the Gunsmith snapped.

"Please, mister . . ."

The Gunsmith quickly aimed his .45 at the man's skull and squeezed the trigger. The echo of the gunshot filled the forest, but the man's cries for mercy ceased.

"But I'm not you," Clint told the corpse at his feet. "Thank God for that . . ."

THE GUNSMITH

26

EAGLE'S GAP

J. R. ROBERTS

CHARTER BOOKS, NEW YORK

THE GUNSMITH #26: EAGLE'S GAP

A Charter Book/published by arrangement with the author

PRINTING HISTORY
Charter Original/March 1984

ISBN: 0-441-30897-X

Charter Books are published by The Berkley Publishing Group,
200 Madison Avenue, New York, N.Y. 10016.
PRINTED IN THE UNITED STATES OF AMERICA

Dedicated to
Patrick E. Andrews

ONE

"Ain't you the feller they call the Gunsmith?" asked a young blonde with big blue eyes and a tempting bow-shaped mouth.

"That's right," the tall slender stranger dressed in denim and trail dust confirmed. "They call me that. I call myself Clint."

"Oh," the girl began. "I didn't figure you'd object to the title, Mr. Adams."

"Hey," Clint began with mock sternness, "I'll grant you I'm a few years older than you, but you don't have to make me feel *that* old. Call me Clint."

"Sure enough," she replied with a smile as lovely as a sunrise on a clear morning.

Clint Adams was indeed a few years older than the girl who worked as a desk clerk for the Wido Hotel. Hell, she couldn't have been more than twenty . . . less than half Clint's age. Of course, the Gunsmith appeared to be ten years younger than he actually was, although the gradual increase of gray in his hair was slowly becoming more prominent.

His physique was lean and fit and his face was ruggedly handsome despite the ten-day-old whisker stubbles on his jaw and the jagged scar marring his left cheek. In fact, the latter seemed to enhance his appearance, adding a quality

1

of intrigue to his features. It certainly hadn't discouraged numerous ladies who found the Gunsmith attractive.

"But why do you object to being called the Gunsmith, Mr.—Clint?" the girl asked. "After all, you are a gunsmith, ain't you?"

"You haven't told me your name, hon," he remarked.

"Libby," the girl replied.

"Okay, Libby," Clint began. "I'm a gunsmith, true enough. I make my living by traveling all over the country, fixing folks' firearms. What gripes me is the fact I was christened 'the Gunsmith' when I was still a deputy sheriff back in Oklahoma. A newspaper man decided to write a story about me because I'd been forced into a couple of gunfights and had to kill the fellas that drew on me."

"Way I heard it," Libby commented, "none of them ever cleared leather."

"Don't you believe it," Clint told her. "Those newspaper fellas always exaggerate things."

He didn't bother to mention that of all the men he'd faced in duels only one had succeeded in drawing his sidearm before the Gunsmith shot him dead.

"So it was one of them newspaper fellers that called you the Gunsmith," the girl said. "Well, I got nothin' against guns. I'm a Texas gal by birth."

"I recognized the accent," Clint said. "I spend a lot of time in the Lone Star state myself."

"What brings you to Idaho?" she asked. "And to a little fly speck of a town like Wido?"

"I've never been here before," Clint replied. "Just happened to drift up this way."

"Glad you did." Libby smiled.

The Gunsmith grinned back at her. Libby was a lovely girl. Her golden hair framed an oval-shaped face with a full mouth, sky-blue eyes and a compact nose. Clint couldn't see much of her figure because the desk blocked his view. He was willing to gamble on that.

"You see," Libby began, reaching under the counter. "I've got a gun here what needs some fixin' done on it."

"Oh," Clint replied lamely, his smile fading.

The girl placed a nickel-plated revolver on the counter; it was a .32-caliber Smith & Wesson.

"The trigger doesn't work," she explained. "Think you can repair it?"

"Sure," Clint answered. "I can have it ready for you by tomorrow morning."

"Thanks, Clint." She smiled.

"What the hell." He shrugged. "It's my job."

TWO

After Clint Adams paid a visit to the saloon and the barbershop, he decided to head over to the livery. As was his custom, the Gunsmith had taken his wagon and horses there before checking into a hotel. Clint paid the hostler double the usual fee to be certain his equipment and animals would be given the best of care.

Especially Duke.

Duke was Clint's most prized possession. A big, beautiful black Arabian gelding, Duke was the strongest, fastest, smartest horse the Gunsmith had ever owned. He would sooner part with his modified double-action Colt—or perhaps even his gun arm—than Duke. The gelding was more than an animal to Clint. Duke was his friend, companion and partner.

Clint felt more presentable, having shaved and bathed and changed to clean clothing. He had also scrounged up enough business to need some tools and parts from his wagon. Besides, he wanted to stop by the livery to check on his property and Duke.

As the Gunsmith reached the stable doors, he heard the familiar whinny of a distressed horse. And not just any horse. He recognized the sound of Duke's whinny as easily as one might the voice of a close friend.

The Gunsmith eased one of the doors open and cautiously peered inside. Two men dressed in tattered old rags that had once been clothes stood at Duke's stall. They were attempting to throw ropes over the horse's head. Duke wasn't being cooperative. He snorted angrily and bobbed his head to avoid the whirling ropes.

Then the gelding reared up on his hind legs. His forelegs shot out like a pugilist's fists. The would-be horse thieves were not as successful at trying to dodge the animal's hooves. An iron-shod foot crashed into the closest man's forehead. The thief fell, his face striped with gushing blood.

"Goddamn crazy hell-horse!" the other thief cried as he bolted away from the stall.

Clint saw the man fumble for a tarnished brass-framed revolver in the waistband of his ragged trousers. The Gunsmith entered the livery and swiftly drew his modified Colt. Snap-aiming, Clint squeezed the trigger.

The report of the Colt roared within the confines of the stable. The horse thief screeched when a 230-grain lead slug struck his elbow. The bullet shattered bone and cartilage in the joint.

"Oh, shit!" the man exclaimed as he clutched his broken arm with his left hand and fell to his knees.

Clint strode to the wounded man, the smoking muzzle of his double-action Colt still trained on the thief. The man stared up at him, tears forming in his pain-filled eyes.

"Jesus, mister," he rasped through clenched teeth. "You didn't have to do that!"

"Yeah," Clint said dryly. "I could have just killed you. Still might unless you take that gun out of your pants and toss it over here."

"That horse belong to you?" the man asked as he followed Clint's instructions.

"Figured that out all by yourself, huh?" Clint muttered, scooping up the man's revolver. It was an old .36-caliber Navy cap-and-ball pistol which looked as if it hadn't been cleaned or oiled since the War Between the States.

"Damned horse is crazy, mister," the thief complained. "It killed Archie, damn it."

The Gunsmith strolled to the stall and glanced down at the man Duke had kicked in the head. Gray bubbles of brains oozed through the crack in the man's forehead. Duke had split the thief's skull.

"Reckon he did at that," Clint commented, holstering his Colt. "Saved the county the price of a trial and the expense of feeding this guy until they hanged him."

"Holy shit!" the surviving thief groaned. "You're a cold-blooded son of a bitch!"

"Penalty for horse stealing is a rope, fella," Clint said simply, patting Duke on the muzzle. The horse uttered a deep-throated murmur of contentment as Clint comforted him. "I didn't make that law, but I can't say I'll mind seeing you swinging on the gallows after you tried to shoot my horse."

"Hell," the thief moaned, "you already shot me. Ain't that enough revenge, for Crissake?"

"You tried to shoot Duke," Clint repeated.

"That was self-defense!"

"Nobody told you to mess with him." The Gunsmith shrugged.

"What in hell is goin' on in here?" an angry voice demanded.

Sheriff Malcolm Kimble stood in the entrance of the livery, a .44 Remington in his fist. A big man with a walrus mustache and a potbelly, Kimble glared at the Gunsmith.

"Adams!" he snapped. "What's the meaning of this?"

The lawman recognized Clint Adams because the Gunsmith had previously paid a visit to the sheriff's office to let Kimble know he was in town. Clint generally did this as a courtesy because he realized the local law likes to know when a stranger is going to be in town for a while—especially one with a reputation as a fast gun.

"And what happened to you, Stu?" Kimble asked, glancing at the wounded man, but his Remington six-shooter was still aimed at Clint. "Appears you been shot."

"This feller's crazy!" the thief declared, pointing a finger at the Gunsmith. "Done shot me for no good reason, Sheriff."

"Well, Adams," Kimble began gruffly, "how come you put a bullet in Stu?"

"He was about to kill my horse—"

"When you came to see me today," Kimble interrupted, "you said you was just here on business. Just traveling through and fixing guns and such, you said. Claimed you wasn't lookin' to make any trouble while you was in Wido."

"I didn't say I'd let some asshole bum try to steal my horse or shoot him 'cause he didn't want to go along with the idea," Clint answered. "Your friend Stu and another varmint he called Archie figured they—"

"Stu ain't exactly a friend of mine," Kimble said quickly, apparently offended by the suggestion. "Him and Archie Bonton are a couple of barflies. They just hang around the saloon, lookin' for a handout and such. They sweep up the place at night and I never knowed them to steal nothin' bigger than a bottle of red-eye."

"They could have bought a lot of whiskey if they stole

Duke and sold him to somebody who appreciates a fine horse," Clint stated.

"Horses sell for less than ten dollars each," Kimble growled. "A good saddle would be easier to steal and sell than a horse. They'd have made a bigger profit too."

"You haven't seen Duke," Clint insisted as he led the animal from the stall.

"Sweet Jesus!" Kimble gasped, staring at the gelding. "Now, that is purely quite a horse, Adams."

Duke was indeed a magnificent animal. The gelding was enormous, almost eighteen hands high and close to nine hundred pounds. Yet Duke was incredibly fit, with the sleek body and long legs of a blooded Arabian. Muscles rippled under his glossy black coat as Duke stepped from the stall.

"I reckon even a couple of dumb bastards like Stu and Archie would figure they could sell a horse like that for a bucket of money," Kimble admitted. He finally holstered his revolver.

"Jesus," Stu gasped. "They'll hang me for this, Sheriff!"

"You should have thought about that before you tried to steal this gent's horse," Kimble told him as he reached down to grab Stu's undamaged arm. "On your feet, Stu. You're under arrest . . ."

Suddenly, Stu swung his left arm, hammering the bottom of his fist into the sheriff's groin. Kimble doubled up with a groan. Stu quickly grabbed the lawman's Remington and yanked it out of leather.

Clint Adams's Colt appeared in his fist faster than Stu could blink an eyelash. He was still fumbling a thumb at the hammer to cock the single-action Remington when Clint fired his gun. A .45 slug drilled through the barfly's heart. Sheriff Kimble awkwardly scrambled away from Stu in revulsion as the man's body convulsed in a hideous spasm of death.

"Damnation," the lawman hissed as he massaged between his legs. "Bastard damn near busted my balls!"

"Don't worry, Sheriff," Clint told him, holstering his Colt. "He won't do it again."

THREE

The Gunsmith didn't have any work left to do by sundown. He had repaired two saddle guns and replaced a broken hammer to a shotgun which belonged to the bartender at the local saloon. Even Sheriff Kimble decided to give Clint some business. He wanted his Remington converted for quick draw. Clint didn't make any radical changes that the sheriff wouldn't be able to handle. He simply put a wider hammer on the revolver and worked on the trigger arm and spring to make the action more smooth without turning it into a hair-trigger.

After eating a steak and potatoes supper in the only diner in Wido, Clint returned to the hotel. Libby was not at the front desk. The Gunsmith sighed with mild disappointment when he saw a sleepy-eyed old man behind the counter instead of the girl.

"Oh, well," he mused as he mounted the stairs, "there'll be other girls—and other towns."

The Gunsmith had already decided it was time to leave Wido. The place wasn't big enough for a traveling gunsmith to make much of a profit. He'd ride out in the morning and head for Eagle's Gap, the next town on his agenda.

At the head of the stairs, Clint stepped into the corridor and located his room. He fished the key from a pocket and prepared to unlock the door. Then he noticed a ribbon of

11

light at the lintel. Clint had not lit the lamp in his room when he'd left earlier that day.

Stepping to the side of the door in case someone lurking inside the room tried to shoot through the door, Clint inserted the key and turned it with his left hand. He drew the Colt with his right. Slowly, he pushed the door open. Clint cautiously peered through the opening, pistol held ready.

"You don't want to kill me, do you?" a feminine voice with an East Texas accent asked softly.

Experience had taught the Gunsmith that a woman can be used as a lure to get a man off guard and set him up for an ambush. Clint had known a couple of women who were deadly enough all by themselves.

However, Clint recognized the girl's voice even as he looked inside and saw Libby waiting for him. The young desk clerk seemed a pretty unlikely choice for a female hootowl. Clint slid his Colt into its holster as he entered the room.

"Howdy, Clint," she greeted. "I shouldn't have used my passkey to get in here, I reckon, but I didn't think you'd mind too much."

"I prefer visitors to knock," Clint told her as he closed the door. "But you're pretty enough to get away with it—this time."

"I'm sorry, Clint," she said. "I thought it would be a nice surprise."

"Oh, it is," the Gunsmith assured her. "But I wouldn't suggest you make a habit of this sort of thing."

"I don't make a habit outta givin' a feller my gun either," Libby replied.

"The Smith & Wesson." Clint nodded. "It needed a new spring. I fixed it earlier today. You want to take it now?"

"You eager for me to leave?" She smiled. "Or just in a hurry to go to bed?"

The Gunsmith raised his eyebrows at the remark. He allowed his gaze to travel over Libby's shapely hour-glass figure. Clint noticed the girl was barefoot, which made him wonder what she had on under her gingham dress.

"I don't want you to leave," Clint told her as he stepped closer and took the girl in his arms.

Their lips pressed together hard, tongues slithering into each other's mouths. Clint ran his fingers along her spine. Libby's hands moved to his chest. She unbuttoned his shirt and slipped her fingers inside.

Clint's mouth moved to the girl's neck, running his tongue along the facial nerve under her jaw. Libby purred with pleasure and gently raked her nails through the mat of dark hair on Clint's chest. The Gunsmith nibbled on her earlobe and slowly shifted his hands to Libby's ribs, gradually moving to her breasts.

"But I would like to go to bed soon," Clint whispered as his thumbs brushed her nipples.

The girl broke the embrace and quickly stripped off her dress. As Clint suspected, she wore nothing underneath. Libby's skin was smooth and creamy white. Her breasts were large and round, capped by pert pink nipples.

The Gunsmith hastily removed his own clothing. Libby inspected his physique with frank admiration. Clint was leanly muscled with a well-developed upper torso, a trim waist and powerful, long legs. The girl hurried to the bed and hopped onto the mattress.

"I don't usually do this, you know," Libby told him. "But Wido ain't very big and we don't have no eligible handsome fellers livin' here. Not many good-lookin' men head through here neither. . . ."

"You don't owe me any explanations, Libby," Clint

assured her as he joined the girl on the bed.

"I just didn't want you to think I'm some sort of whore, you know," she said sheepishly.

"I don't think anything of the kind," the Gunsmith stated, stroking the girl's golden hair. "A woman has needs just like a man does. That's natural enough. I'm not one to find fault with that."

"Thanks, Clint," she said with relief, placing a hand on his chest.

"But I'd better tell you something," he began. "Just so we understand each other."

"I'm listening," Libby replied solemnly.

"I'm going to be moving on tomorrow," Clint told her. "It's just not my way to stay any place for long. I'll be on my way in the morning."

"I didn't reckon you was fixin' to marry me, Clint," Libby laughed. "Don't worry none 'bout hurtin' my feelin's because you're leavin' tomorrow. Just give me somethin' to remember tonight."

The Gunsmith was determined to do exactly that. He skillfully ran his hands over Libby's body. The girl sighed and cooed as he massaged her breasts. His hands moved along her belly while he kissed her breasts, licking the erect nipples.

Libby found Clint's stiff manhood and pulled gently, fondling the length of his penis. The Gunsmith felt the fire in his loins increase as Libby stroked him faster and faster.

The Gunsmith's hands moved to Libby's thighs, rubbing his fingertips on the soft warm flesh. He found her tawny wet portal and inserted two fingers. She moaned as he moved his hand to and fro.

"Ohhh, Clint," Libby urged. "Do it now!"

Clint mounted her. Libby spread her legs wide and helped steer his hard member between her thighs. He felt himself enter her, his hungry cock sinking inside the warm dampness. Libby gasped as he began to rotate his hips, gradually working himself deeper.

The girl bucked beneath Clint. He continued to drive himself into her, pumping his buttocks, steadily increasing the motion as he felt the girl approach an orgasm. The Gunsmith thrust harder until Libby convulsed in primitive erotic ecstasy.

Clint was tempted to keep pumping until he relieved his own burning desire as well. The Gunsmith resisted the urge and once again repeated the gradual grinding of hips to stimulate the girl once more. Soon, Libby's nails raked his back. She gasped and trembled as she journeyed to paradise a second time.

Clint joined her. He released his load, shooting the hot seed inside Libby. He rested on top of her, bracing himself on his elbows. Libby hummed happily and embraced his neck.

"Now, that was purely somethin' to remember," she told him.

"For both of us," the Gunsmith whispered in reply.

Then they continued to make the night even more memorable.

FOUR

When Clint Adams awoke the following morning, Libby had already gotten out of bed and dressed. She'd found her S&W .32 in a desk drawer and put the pistol in her handbag.

"I'd better go, Clint," Libby told him as she headed for the door. "Thanks for everything."

The Gunsmith was glad that Libby hadn't insisted on dragging out the affair. He didn't want emotional attachments of any kind. Clint had always found love to be a path to pain, disappointment and shattered dreams.

After Libby left, Clint dressed, gathered up his belongings and checked out of the hotel. As he headed for the stable his stomach growled, reminding him that he had eaten supper several hours before spending an energetic night with Libby.

"What the hell," Clint muttered, glancing at the diner.

Although the Gunsmith spent most of his time on the trail, he still favored a sit-down meal to eating the canned sardines, tomatoes and jerky which comprised the bulk of his diet while he traveled from town to town. Those bland meals would come soon enough, so he decided to enjoy a proper breakfast before he left Wido.

The restaurant was empty when Clint entered. He selected a table and sat with his back to the wall and facing

17

the door. It was a habit he had acquired long ago—one of many which had helped him survive over the years.

There were half a dozen tables with checkered cloths and chairs, but no waitress was on duty. Then he gazed out a window. A group of townsfolk were gathered around a brick building. He vaguely heard the murmur of their jumbled conversation. Some of the people looked up at the building roof while others glanced down at the ground. Others just shook their heads with dismay.

The Gunsmith craned his neck to get a look at the legend above the open doors of the place. It was the Wido Bank. Clint frowned, wondering what was going on.

"Oh, howdy there—Mr. Adams, ain't it?" a woman with a rather gruff voice inquired.

"That's right," Clint replied, looking up to see a portly, middle-aged waitress cross the room to his table.

"Figured that's who you was," she remarked. "Everybody heard 'bout how you had to kill those no-good drunkards Stu Collins and Archie Bonton yesterday."

"I didn't kill Archie," Clint explained. "My horse did."

"Then you give your horse a sugar cube as a reward," the waitress said. "Town is better off without those two. Not fit examples for our younguns to see, I say. Hear you saved the sheriff's life too."

"Not exactly . . ." the Gunsmith began.

"Well, I won't hold that against you, Mr. Adams." She shrugged. "Fact is, this town could surely use a new sheriff. Don't suppose you'd be interested in the job, would you?"

"I'm leaving town right after breakfast."

"Oh, Lord!" the waitress huffed. "Reckon I'd best take your order instead of jawin' away when you want to eat."

"I'll have some scrambled eggs, sausage, potatoes and coffee, ma'am."

"We'll fix it for you pronto, Mr. Adams." The woman nodded.

"That'll be fine, ma'am," Clint assured her.

"You can just call me Milly."

"And you can call me Clint, Milly." He smiled. "By the way, do you happen to know what all the fuss is about over at the bank?"

"Surely do, Clint," Milly replied. "Somebody went and robbed it last night. Purely glad I didn't keep no money in that bank. Never trusted banks nohow."

"The bank was robbed?" The Gunsmith raised his eyebrows with surprise. "I sleep pretty light, but I didn't hear a thing last night. How'd they do it?"

"Appears somebody knocked a hole in the roof and just climbed down inside, Milly answered.

"Sheriff Kimble has some deputies, doesn't he? Wasn't anybody on duty last night? Fella should have heard something."

"Deputy Carter was on duty," Milly confirmed. "Poor feller. Just got married last month too. Gonna be mighty hard on his wife."

"You mean he's dead?" Clint asked, startled by the fact a lawman was killed silently in the middle of the night. "I'm sure I would have heard a shot. Did somebody knife him?"

-"Sheriff ain't sure how it was done." Milly sighed. "But Willy Carter is dead and our bank was robbed, sure enough."

"I'll be . . ." Clint whispered. "Must be some unusual thieves. I guess the sheriff is putting together a posse out there."

"Don't see what good that'll do." Milly shrugged. "Bank robbers didn't leave no tracks."

"What?" Clint wasn't certain he'd heard the waitress correctly. "They didn't leave any tracks? But how did they get on the roof or leave with the money?"

"Don't rightly know, Clint," Milly answered. "Would you like some coffee now?"

"Yeah." The Gunsmith nodded, absentmindedly staring out the window at the bank.

"There you are, Adams," the voice of Sheriff Kimble declared when the lawman entered the diner half an hour later.

"Morning, Sheriff," Clint replied as he finished his eggs and sausage. "Care for a cup of coffee?"

The lawman nodded. "That's to my taste."

"Milly?" the Gunsmith called to the waitress. "Can we have another cup and a fresh pot of coffee?"

"Surely, Clint," she replied, casting a distasteful glance at Kimble.

"Reckon you heard 'bout what happened," the sheriff commented to Clint.

"Yeah." The Gunsmith nodded. "Sorry to hear about your deputy. How'd it happen?"

"Doc Sterling looked over Willy's body and he still ain't sure." Kimble sighed. "Appears Willy got punctured clean through his chest. There's a hole in his back."

"Punctured?"

"That's right," the lawman confirmed. "Weren't no knife or even a sword done it. Looks almost like a bullet wound, but there ain't no way to fire a gun without no noise . . . is there?"

"Nobody has invented anything that I know of," Clint replied. "Not yet."

"The Doc says the closest thing the wound resembles is

an arrow wound,'' Kimble stated. "Except it ain't messy enough. A flint or iron-headed hunting arrow makes a mighty nasty exit hole.''

"What about this business that the robbers didn't leave any footprints?'' the Gunsmith asked.

"That's a fact, Adams,'' Kimble answered. "No hoof or boot prints anywhere near the bank to explain how it was done. No fresh tracks heading out of Wido neither.''

"Any by the deputy's body?''

"One set of footprints,'' Kimble said. "Mighty funny lookin' tracks too. Old Orly Saunders looked 'em over. Orly used to be an Indian guide for the cavalry. He knows how to read sign better than any man in the county, but he couldn't help us none. He can't figure this out no way. Orly's sure the thieves didn't cover up their tracks. *They just didn't leave none.*''

"Except for the footprints by the deputy's body,'' Clint reminded him.

"That ain't no help,'' Kimble muttered. "Orly says the feller who made them tracks had sort of normal-sized feet. He was wearin' some sort of funny footgear. Not boots, cause the print isn't deep enough. More like bedroom slippers or something like that.''

"How about moccasins?'' Clint suggested.

"Orly doesn't think so.''

"Well, Sheriff,'' the Gunsmith said with a sigh, "I guess you've got yourself one hell of a mystery to unravel.''

"Tell me somethin' I ain't already figured out, Adams,'' Kimble growled sourly.

FIVE

"Hell, Sheriff"—Clint shrugged—"what do you want from me? I didn't rob the bank or kill your deputy."

"Didn't figure you had," Kimble assured him, sipping his coffee. "But I've heard tell you've solved some mighty puzzling crimes in your day."

"Maybe my day is over," the Gunsmith replied dryly.

"You caught them murderers in Willow Falls and Two Queens, didn't you?"

"Yeah," Clint admitted. "But nobody figured those killers were ghosts."

"Didn't you tangle with that Mex bandit they called the Ghost?"

"*El Espectro.*" Clint nodded. "I'm not likely to forget him. But that son of a bitch turned out to be made of flesh and blood just like the—"

The Gunsmith almost mentioned the sasquatch.* Six months before riding into Wido he had gotten involved with a pair of British scientists who were trying to capture the Indian spirit that was said to be half man and half beast. The incident had been too bizarre to talk about . . . unless Clint wanted folks to figure he was loco.

*The Gunsmith #21: Sasquatch Hunt

"Like the other varmints I've met," he concluded.

"Well," Kimble said. "I'd sort of hoped you might be willing to give me a hand with this."

"Sheriff," the Gunsmith began wearily. "I've got a powerful curious streak, I admit. I also admit that it's gotten me in more trouble than I would have had in the past if I'd chosen to keep my nose out of matters that didn't directly involve me until I butted in like a damned fool."

"That's understandable, Adams. Just figured you might care that Deputy Carter was killed in cold blood, what with you havin' once been a lawman yourself and all . . ."

"Aw, shit," Clint muttered. "Let me finish my coffee. Then we'll take a look at this supernatural crime of yours."

The Gunsmith and Sheriff Kimble walked to the bank. Clint glanced down at the ground. The dirt was covered with an assortment of footprints. He clucked his tongue with disgust.

"Reckon the town had a picnic here, Sheriff?" Clint remarked dryly.

"No sense in keeping them away after Orly already checked the spot for tracks," Kimble replied. "I seen for myself, Adams. Believe me, there wasn't so much as a fresh footprint here."

"And I suppose the slipper-prints or whatever they were have been trampled by now as well," Clint commented.

"Didn't pay them much mind when we carried Willy's body over to the doc's office," the sheriff admitted. "But we kept everybody away until Orly got a look at them."

"Okay," Clint began, "where is this tracking marvel?"

"Orly owns the local tannery," Kimble answered. "I'll take you there."

Orly Saunders was busy stitching together a leather belt when Clint and Kimble entered his shop. A scrawny, wrinkled old man with an unkempt white beard and surly, squinty eyes, Orly looked up sharply at the pair.

"What do ye want o' me now, Sheriff?" he demanded gruffly.

"Orly," Kimble began, "this feller is Clint Adams—"

"Great day in the morning!" Orly exclaimed. "Why I heard tell 'bout ye from Bill Hickok. Pity that yeller polecat done shot Jim in the back. Purely glad they finally hanged that bastard like 'n he had comin' to him. Jim was a mighty good man an' he always talked well o' ye, Clint Adams."

"A pleasure to meet you, Orly," the Gunsmith said as he shook hands with the old man.

"Pleasure is all mine, Clint." Orly smiled. "I disremember when I been more pleased to meet a feller."

"Sheriff tells me you're quite a tracker, Orly," the Gunsmith said. "But you couldn't figure out the sign the bank robbers left."

"There ain't no sign, Clint," Orly insisted. "Looky here, young feller. Wild Bill would 'a vouched for me bein' able to read sign, but there ain't nothin' there."

"Okay." Clint nodded. "You're the expert. I sure as hell don't qualify. How about those slipper prints?"

"That's 'bout all I can tell ye." Orly shrugged.

"You can tell us more than that, friend," Clint insisted. "You're an expert. Tell us a few things about our killer."

Orly grinned. "Ye know 'bout us trackers, don't ye?"

"Enough to appreciate the fact you can tell a lot by looking at a man's footprints."

"That's a fact, son," Orly confirmed. "Them slipper tracks was made by a feller what weighed maybe a hundred and fifty pounds. Walked kinda light, favored the balls o' his feet. If'n his feet match the rest o' him, and I figure they do, the feller ye want is probably 'bout five foot six and pretty strong. Them tracks was made by muscular feet."

"From the way the prints were positioned," Clint began, "do you think the killer jammed some sort of short spear through Deputy Carter's chest and then pulled it out after he killed him?"

"Come to think on it," Orly's squinty eyes widened, "there wasn't enough dirt shifted around them tracks for that."

"How's this for a theory?" Clint mused. "Maybe somebody threw a lance or fired some sort of arrow into the deputy and the slipper-man yanked it out of his chest?"

"That makes sense." Orly nodded. " 'Cept for one thing."

"What's that?"

"Weren't no footprints of this slipper-feller 'cept right there by Willy's body." Orly shrugged. "Reckon maybe the killer done *flew* over to Willy's corpse?"

"I reckon not," the Gunsmith muttered.

Clint Adams entered the bank vault and stared up at the hole in the ceiling. It was roughly four feet in diameter. The crumbled chunks of adobe brick lay in a crude heap on the floor.

"They punched a hole through the roof and climbed

down right into the vault," the Gunsmith remarked, unable to keep a trace of admiration from his tone. "Clever sons of bitches."

"What the hell did they use?" Sheriff Kimble wondered. "Regular pickaxes couldn't have done that."

"Not without waking up the whole town," Clint agreed. He turned to the bank president, Douglas Jacobs. "How much money did you have in this vault?"

"About fifteen thousand dollars," Jacobs answered. "See, this is the only bank in the county. We get business from all over. Lot of farmers. They like to get that interest and they know they might need to borrow from the bank in the future if their crops do poorly."

Clint examined a row of metal doors which had been forced open by a crowbar. "These must be safety deposit boxes, right?"

"Yes, sir," the banker confirmed. "There were all sorts of valuables in there. Jewelry, rare gold coins, even a couple silver ingots from some Nevada miners who moved to Idaho last year."

"Anybody make a deposit recently?" Clint asked. "Perhaps somebody who insisted on coming into the vault to see his valuables locked in the safety deposit box?"

Jacobs nodded. "Why, yes. Only two days ago. A foreigner, gentleman named Mancini, brought in an emerald necklace. He claimed it was a family heirloom."

"And where was this man supposed to be staying?" Clint asked.

"With some friends outside of town," Jacobs answered. "The Maynard family, I believe."

"Maynard and his family are at Culpepper City to attend his brother's wedding," Kimble stated. "They left five days ago and ain't due back until next week."

"The place is empty?" Clint asked.

"A couple hired hands is still there," the sheriff replied.

"Maybe we should check on the Maynard place," Clint suggested. "And have a talk with Mr. Mancini."

Clint and Sheriff Kimble rode to the Maynard spread, a small potato farm about five miles outside of Wido. As they approached the farmhouse, Clint loosened the retaining thong from the hammer of his Colt .45 in case he had to use it in a hurry. They brought their mounts to a halt in front of the house. The lawman tied the reins of his Morgan to the hitching rail. Clint let Duke remain free, confident the gelding wouldn't wander off.

"Jed? Harry?" Kimble called as he stepped onto the porch. "You fellers around here?"

When he knocked on the door it swung open. Kimble and Clint stared inside. Two men dressed in dirty denim lay on the floor. Their hands had been tied behind their backs and their ankles bound together. Crusty brown stains of dried blood surrounded their throats—which had been cut wide open from ear to ear.

"Sweet Jesus protect us," the sheriff whispered with a choked gasp.

"They've been dead for some time," Clint observed. "I don't think you'll find their killer hanging around here now."

"You figure it was this Mancini feller?" Kimble asked, tilting his head at the corpses.

"I don't think the killer's real name is Mancini," Clint replied. "He's too smart to give his real name. But whoever the bastard really is, he's responsible for killing these two men and your deputy, as well as robbing the bank."

"Wonderful," Kimble muttered. "But how do I find the son of a bitch?"

"Sheriff," the Gunsmith said, sighing, "I have no idea."

SIX

The mysterious events that had taken place at Wido and the Maynard farm ate at Clint Adams's thoughts as he rode his wagon along the flat grassy terrain of the Idaho wilderness. He had been sorely tempted to remain and help Sheriff Kimble with the investigation, but there was no point to that. The mysterious Mr. Mancini and whoever assisted him had clearly already vanished.

Clint didn't envy Kimble. How was he going to explain any of this to the people of Wido? What would he say when the farmer and his family returned to find their hired hands had been murdered while they attended a wedding? Bad news, Maynard. Your men were killed and I don't have a damned idea who did it. Bank was robbed too. By the way, you plan to vote for me come election day?

The Gunsmith had been a lawman for eighteen years, long enough to be furious when a criminal appeared to have escaped scot-free and there wasn't a single clue to suggest where the hell he ran to. Still, Clint realized he couldn't do anything about it. He had a living to earn and hanging around Wido holding the sheriff's hand wouldn't do anyone any good.

"Well, big fella," Clint called back at Duke who followed the rig, loosely tied to a guideline, "you're so damn smart, maybe you can figure out how they did it."

31

The gelding snorted in reply.

"That's what I figured." The Gunsmith sighed. "Me neither."

One of the team horses uttered a snort, imitating Duke. Clint clucked his tongue.

"Don't you guys gang up on me," he complained. "We're heading to Eagle's Gap to try to drum up some more business. Gotta keep you fellas in oats, don't I? What happened in Wido isn't my worry and I don't intend to ride back there now. Nothing I can do about it anyway, so—"

Suddenly, he noticed something move among the trees of a forest located a couple hundred yards from the trail. He barely glimpsed a flash of pale pink between two trunks. Clint stared at the trees until he spotted the shape again.

The figure was a handsome woman. Clint was certain he recognized the form of round breasts and the comely curves of feminine hips and legs. She darted from one tree to another. The Gunsmith hadn't gotten a very good look, but he could have sworn the girl was naked.

"I'll be a cross-eyed horntoad," he whispered in awe. "All of this *can't* be happening to me in *one day*."

"Mister!" a woman's voice cried hoarsely. "Help!"

The nymph emerged from the treeline and jogged toward Clint's wagon. She was a lovely young girl, not more than twenty years old. Her fantastic body was well displayed as she ran for the Gunsmith, her knees buckling as she clearly pushed herself beyond exhaustion.

However, despite the previous impression, the girl was not naked. She wore pink tights, the likes of which Clint had never seen outside of a carnival. *What the hell is she doing running around out here dressed like that?* he wondered.

"Help, mister!" she pleaded. "They're after me!"

Before Clint could react two figures on horseback burst from the treeline behind the girl. They galloped after her in determined pursuit. Clint saw one of them aim a strange weapon, which looked familar although he could not identify it from a distance. The horseman aimed his weapon at the girl.

"Down!" Clint shouted as he yanked back the reins to bring his team to a halt.

The girl dove to the ground. The *twang* of a taut cord unleashed and the *hiss* of a projectile followed. The horseman had fired his odd device, which resembled a rifle without a barrel. A wooden shaft jutted from the ground less than a foot from the girl's sprawled form.

Clint glanced at the second horseman who continued to advance while his partner stopped his mount and hastily leaped from the saddle. The advancing figure also held the same type of weapon. Clint noticed an arched strip of flexible wood across the front of the stock.

"Holy shit!" he exclaimed. "It's a crossbow!"

The killer, dressed in a checkered shirt and a Montana peaked hat and mounted on a brown and white piebald, looked like he'd be more at home with a Winchester instead of an antique weapon. Outdated or not, Clint realized the crossbow was designed to fire a metal-tipped bolt accurately up to five hundred feet, which was a longer range than he could manage with a six-gun. And the horseman was aiming the crossbow at him.

The Gunsmith leaped from the wagon as the *twang-hiss* of the second crossbow filled his ears. Metal struck wood solidly. A wooden bolt was lodged in the footboard of the wagon, its feathered end vibrating from the impact of its metal tip biting into wood hard.

The horseman kept coming. He tossed the crossbow

aside and drew a revolver from a hip holster as he closed in. The Gunsmith nodded, pleased that the attacker had now chosen to take him on with a weapon which Clint had mastered. The killer fired his pistol first. Dirt spat up from the ground almost a yard from the Gunsmith's feet.

Clint waited until the attacker was within range. He raised his modified Colt in a two-hand grip and squeezed the trigger twice. The double-action six-gun snarled and two .45 bullets smashed into the horseman's chest. Blood splashed his checkered shirt before his body toppled out of the saddle.

The first assailant remained on his feet, using his roan gelding for cover. Clint saw the man poke the snout of his crossbow between the legs of his horse. The Gunsmith hit the dirt and rolled away from his wagon. Another bolt sizzled through the air and slammed into the body panel of the Gunsmith's rig.

Clint leaped to his feet and rushed his opponent's position, aware that a crossbow must be reloaded after each bolt is fired.

The Gunsmith dashed toward his adversary who was hastily trying to pull back the bowstring. The killer inserted a bolt along the grooved top of the stock and raised the crossbow as Clint rapidly closed in. He aimed the weapon at Clint and prepared to pull the trigger.

The modified Colt roared. Wood splintered from the frame of the crossbow as a .45 slug smashed into it. The weapon hurled from the hands of its stunned owner. The killer reacted instantly, his hand streaking for a six-gun in a belly holster.

Clint fired his Colt once more. The assailant's head recoiled violently as a bullet drilled through his forehead and blasted out the back of his skull. The enemy horseman collapsed to the ground. He died too quickly to utter a sound.

"Oh, thank God," the girl gasped as she rose to her feet. "They would have killed me for sure if you hadn't showed up, mister."

"It's over now, ma'am," the Gunsmith assured her, opening the loading gate of his Colt to replace the spent cartridges with fresh shells. "You'll be okay."

"I just can't thank you enough for what you've done. . . ."

"Well, lady," Clint remarked, "a lot of strange things have been happening lately. I'd sure like to hear an explanation for some of them."

"It's a long story, mister." the girl sighed wearily.

"I'm a slow eater," the Gunsmith replied. "You can tell me about it over dinner."

SEVEN

"My name's Jane Harlow," the girl began as she sat beside Clint by the campfire.

"I'm Clint Adams," he told her.

The Gunsmith gazed at the young woman's face in the yellow light of the fire. Her hair was pale blond, almost white. Wide hazel eyes peered out from her lean face, highlighted by high cheekbones. He hadn't really looked at her face until that moment because her costume offered such a stunning display of her body.

"Reckon I'd better get you a blanket, Jane. Might get a bit chilly."

"Thank you, Mr. Adams."

"Call me Clint," he urged. "And tell me why you're dressed in pink tights and had to run away from a couple fellas armed with crossbows, of all things."

"I apologize for the costume," Jane said sheepishly.

"Honey," Clint said with a grin. "You don't have anything to apologize for."

"I'll take that as a compliment," she replied, unable to resist a smile.

"No other way for a pretty lady to take that sort of comment."

Having found a blanket in the back of his wagon, Clint handed it to the girl and then joined her by the fire. Then he opened a can of beans and poured them into a frying pan.

"Okay," he said as he tore some beef jerky into pieces and added it to the beans, "why don't you tell me how all this happened?"

"I joined the circus."

"A circus?" Clint asked, pouring freshly brewed coffee into two tin cups. He gave one to the girl.

"You see," Jane began, "my folks were circus people themselves before they decided to get married and raise a family. They settled in Idaho and ran a dairy farm, but they couldn't quite get the sawdust out of their system. Mother taught my sister and me some acrobatics and ever since I was a little girl, I wanted to be a circus performer, although our folks told us it wasn't a good profession to get into."

"So you ran way from home to join the circus?"

"Not exactly," Jane said. "Our mother died from pneumonia and father had a fatal heart attack about a year later. Martha and I ran the farm for a while, but I got restless to see the world. Finally, I moved to Summit Falls."

The girl stared up at the twilight sky and pulled the blanket around herself. Clint allowed her to tell the story at her own speed and continued to prepare their dinner.

"Well, I got bored working at a general store too," Jane said. "I was trying to decide whether to find another job or return home. Then the Circus Incredible came to town. They didn't have a female acrobat so I got hired pretty easy."

"But you decided to quit and your employer sent a couple of killers after you?" Clint frowned. "There must be more to it than that."

"You figure I stole from Feltrinelli or something like that?" she demanded.

"I don't even know who this Felt—Feltrinelli?—is."

"He's the owner of the Circus Incredible," she explained. "He was a famous acrobat back in Italy until he had an accident that crippled him for life. Maybe that warped his mind, I don't know. I do know he's a thief and a murderer. That circus of his is a traveling band of criminals. Everybody in it is wanted for crimes committed in this country or Europe. You've never seen such a collection of cutthroats."

"What sort of cutthroats?" Clint asked, shoveling beans into two plates.

"Thieves, murderers, sex perverts." Jane shook her head. "I was raped so many times it's a wonder I didn't bleed to death."

"How long did you have to go through all this?" Clint asked, handing her a plate of beans.

"About five months," she replied. "It seemed more like five years. I finally got a chance to escape when they were busy with one of the balloons late last night."

"Balloons?" Clint raised his eyebrows.

"Hot air balloons," the girl explained. "You know the type. They haul baskets big enough to carry people into the sky. Feltrinelli and several of his men are trained aeronauts. That's what they call balloon pilots."

"They used these balloons as part of the circus performances?"

"Sure," Jane replied. "They sell rides on those things. Folks pay a nickel for a chance to fly for a few minutes. They also use the balloons for a trapeze act performed by the Feltrinelli Brothers—who are the circus master's sons."

"Hold on a minute," the Gunsmith said. "You said they were busy with the balloon late last night. Was that for a performance or had they used it for a personal trip of some sort?"

"I think they used it to commit a crime," Jane answered. "They didn't tell me any more than they had to about their illegal activities."

"Would this balloon happen to be a dark color?" Clint asked. "Would it blend with the night?"

"Damn right it would," she confirmed. "The airship they flew off in last night was *The Black Moon*. It's entirely black—the balloon, the basket, even the sandbags and ropes. From a distance it looks like a dark cloud in the night sky."

"I think I know how somebody slips into a town in the middle of the night and robs a bank without leaving any tracks to suggest which way they went," Clint commented.

"What are you talking about?" the puzzled girl asked.

The Gunsmith explained about the baffling robbery of the Wido Bank and the multiple murders that had occurred in the town.

"The thieves could have floated into town in the balloon and positioned the craft over the bank," Clint said. "Then these acrobat crooks climbed down ropes and broke through the roof."

"The iron drill!" Jane declared. "They have a big drill like some mining companies use. It was attached to the bottom of the basket of *The Black Moon*."

"Those drills can bite through solid rock," Clint mused. "It could have punctured the roof of that bank. The thieves would probably have had to widen the hole with pickaxes, but that wouldn't have been too difficult after the drill did its work. Then they just dropped into the vault. Of course, they knew exactly where the vault was located thanks to the visit by 'Mr. Mancini' beforehand.''

"And I'll tell you who that was,'' Jane added. ''Feltrinelli himself. He and some of his goons left our camp a couple days ago. He can be very charming and dignified, just the sort to convince a banker that he was a fine gentleman from Europe.''

"Yeah,'' Clint agreed as he gathered up one of the crossbows he'd confiscated from its lifeless owner. ''And I know how Deputy Carter was killed too. They used one of these. Then an acrobat was lowered down by a rope and pulled the bolt out of the dead lawman. That explains the footprints too. Circus acrobats wear thin slippers, like the pair you have on.''

"I don't know for sure what happened last night,'' Jane said. ''But they were plenty pleased with the loot they brought back from their midnight balloon flight. They were so busy unloading it, I figured they wouldn't notice if I made my break.''

"Apparently they noticed you were gone later,'' Clint remarked. ''How many men does Feltrinelli have working for him?''

"Enough to send more than two men after me,'' the girl replied grimly.

"That's a pleasant thought.'' The Gunsmith sighed.

EIGHT

After the meal, Clint Adams poured the last of the coffee into their cups and shoveled dirt onto the fire to extinguish it. He sat beside Jane Harlow and watched smoke curl from the smoldering ashes.

"No sense in advertising where we are," the Gunsmith explained.

"If Bolo is tracking me," Jane whispered, "it won't make any difference."

"Even the best trackers have trouble reading sign after dark," Clint told her.

"Bolo doesn't have to see a trail," the girl said. "He can *smell* a person's scent like a hunting dog."

"Hell, Jane," Clint said, slipping an arm around her shoulders, "they just told you that crap to scare you into thinking you couldn't escape."

"You don't know Bolo," she insisted. "He's not human."

"I know that a man isn't a bloodhound," Clint replied. "And I know its been more than three hours since we sent those two bastards to Boot Hill and nobody else has showed up. That means those two were probably the only men Feltrinelli has sent so far."

"I suppose you're right, Clint," she said, snuggling against his chest. "Besides, I feel safe with you."

43

"You *are* safe," he assured her. "Come sun up, we'll move on to the nearest town—Eagle's Gap—"

"Eagle's Gap!" Jane's hazel eyes widened. "My sister lives there!"

"Well, how about that?" Clint grinned. "You're heading home."

"What will we do about Feltrinelli's circus?" she asked.

"Don't worry about that," Clint replied, stroking Jane's pale blond hair. "The Circus Incredible won't be too hard for the federal marshals to find. With our combined testimony we'll have enough proof to get them to launch an investigation. We can contact Sheriff Kimble in Wido to add further support if we have to. When the feds raid the circus, they'll find enough to put Feltrinelli and his people behind bars—if not on the gallows."

"Thank God," she whispered. "It'll all be over soon."

"Yeah," Clint replied softly, kissing her on the forehead. "What are you going to do after you get home?"

"I'll have time to figure that out later," Jane said, gazing up at him. "I'm interested in what we're going to do tonight."

She closed her eyes and parted her lips slightly. The Gunsmith accepted the invitation, pressing his mouth to hers. He drank in the kiss, lingering the contact, savoring her taste.

Gradually, their hands moved to explore each other's body. Clint slid his fingers down her torso, gently fondling her breasts. Jane's nipples were erect and firm under his skillful touch. The girl found his stiff manhood and began to unbutton his trousers.

The Gunsmith's hands moved lower. He stroked her long, shapely thighs, clad only in the thin silk tights. His fingers probed at her moist womanhood as the girl freed his hard, throbbing cock.

Jane's head descended to his crotch. Clint moaned with pleasure as she closed her lips around his fleshy shaft. The girl drew on him slowly, riding the length of his penis as her head moved up and down in a gradually faster tempo.

Clint began to near the brink. Jane realized this and released him. She quickly stripped off her flimsy costume. The Gunsmith followed her example. Naked, they once again fell into each other's arms.

"Lie down, darling," Jane urged in a husky, passionate voice. "Let me show you what Utopia is all about."

Clint lay back on a blanket, the night breeze brushing his hot skin. Jane straddled him, her breasts bouncing slightly as she seized his manhood. The girl guided his member into her warm, eager womb.

Neither of them noticed Duke's disturbed snort as the animal sniffed at the air, trying to detect an unfamiliar scent carried by the wind.

The Gunsmith and Jane gasped as the coupling began. Her womanhood seemed to grasp him like a damp fist. He reached forward and traced his fingertips along her breasts, plucking gently at the stiff nipples. Jane smiled as she began to rock back and forth.

The girl slowly increased the motion and Clint arched his back to the tempo of her movements. His buttocks pressed against the ground hard as he lunged deeper into her center of love. Jane moaned happily and bounced up and down, riding his manhood to glory.

Clint pounded away faster and harder. The couple nearly reached a frenzy of erotic delight, their naked flesh clapping together in their energetic efforts. Then their joyous passionate labors reached a mutual pinnacle of endurance.

Jane cried out as an uncontrollable orgasm swept through her. Clint gasped and groaned, blasting his load into her chamber of love. The girl panted and trembled, still seated on his crotch, their sexes entwined.

"God," she whispered. "It's been so long since I've done this because I *wanted* to. It's even better than I remembered it was."

"It can be one of the best things in life," the Gunsmith told her. "One of the very best."

"It couldn't get much better," the girl agreed.

She leaned down and kissed him gently on the mouth. Clint's hands traveled along her ribs to her hips; before long the fires of desire burned once more and the couple began to make love again.

Then Duke reared up on his hind legs and brayed an unmistakable call of alarm. Clint didn't fail to recognize his horse's warning and he realized that Duke's sense of danger was infallible.

"Somebody's out there," the Gunsmith declared as he abruptly withdrew from Jane.

"Oh, God," she gasped, half in fear and half because he had detached himself so suddenly.

Clint rolled to the pile of clothing and reached for his gunbelt. His hand closed around the grips of his modified .45 Colt revolver as he heard bushes rustle from a large body brushing through them. The Gunsmith yanked the pistol from leather.

He heard the sinister song of a crossbow string followed by the brief sizzle of a bolt in flight. Then the sickening smack of steel and wood piercing flesh filled his ears. Jane Harlow groaned in pain.

"No!" Clint shouted angrily as he turned to face the girl.

She stood unsteadily, eyes wide with disbelief. Her

mouth opened and closed without uttering a sound. Both hands were fisted around the slender wooden shaft that extended from her left breast.

Jane stared down at the crossbow bolt buried in her chest. She looked to Clint, her eyes filled with pleading and pain. Blood seeped over her breast, dying the flesh crimson. Jane tried to speak, but only a grisly rattle of death escaped from her throat.

Then she toppled to the ground and died.

"You murdering bastards!" Clint snarled, swinging his pistol toward the trees.

The Gunsmith didn't enjoy killing. He had never found pleasure in the taking of another person's life. Yet at that moment, he wanted to kill. He wanted to see the murderers of Jane Harlow thrashing on the ground with their guts spilling out from bullet holes. He wanted to hear them beg for mercy, plead for him to terminate their suffering with a fast death from a .45 round in the brain.

"You bastards want a fight?" he challenged. "Come and get it!"

But silence was their only reply.

NINE

"No stomach for a real fight, eh?" the Gunsmith shouted. "Well, you scummy sons of bitches better run fast and hide real good because—"

He stopped before he could continue wasting energy on meaningless threats. His temper had gotten the better of his reason. One doesn't alert an enemy to trouble. One simply goes after them. And kills them.

The Colt .45 still in his fist and his eyes still trained on the surrounding trees, Clint reached for his clothes. As he gathered up his trousers a small pistol dropped from his pants and landed on his shirt and boots which still lay on the ground.

"Get a hold of yourself, Adams," he chided himself. "You'd feel pretty stupid if you killed yourself with your own hideout gun, for God's sake."

The Gunsmith hastily stepped into his trousers and pulled up his pants, still watching the forest. He tried to detect any warning sound of danger, but the woods remained silent. Duke and the other horses did not stir, aware their master was ready to take care of the situation.

Yet, their silence itself warned Clint that the unseen assailants had not retreated.

Suddenly, something whirled from the treeline.

Clint nearly dove to the ground in response, but the

projectile didn't head in his direction. He caught a glimpse of a spinning shape which sailed around the camp in a wide arc. The disc totally baffled him.

Then, abruptly and without warning, it changed course and flew straight for his unprotected skull.

Taken completely off guard, the Gunsmith's reflexes were still extraordinary and he almost managed to dodge the whirling weapon. Almost. Something hard cracked against the side of his head, just above the left temple. Lights exploded behind his eyes and he felt his legs turn to water.

The Gunsmith crashed to the ground. He stared up at the night sky, gazing through a blurry mist. Something dug into the small of his back. The shape seemed familiar. Clint realized he was lying on top of his own clothes and the New Line hideout gun.

Gun, his mind said sternly. *The gun.*

His right hand flexed, but the modified .45 revolver was no longer there.

Clint tried to sit up, his head spinning like a top, his stomach knotting up and his heart racing. His vision cleared suddenly and he saw a hideous apparition emerge from the trees.

The creature resembled a man, tall and leanly muscled with dark skin and a bushy head of black hair. Naked except for a loincloth, the walking nightmare could have been a primitive demon summoned by some sort of prehistoric necromancy.

It gazed down at Clint. The creature's face was lean with a huge nose and flaring nostrils and wide, rubbery lips. The eyes were all but invisible slits in a nut brown face although the brows were very shaggy. An unkept black beard covered its jaw and a network of strange circular scars formed twin stripes on its cheeks.

A bright green stone was attached to the side of its nose, fixed somehow above the left nostril. The man-beast looked at the Gunsmith with disinterest and stooped to pick up an odd-looking piece of curved wood.

"You get the girl, Bolo," a voice declared. "I'll take care of this son of a bitch."

A second figure approached as the creature moved to the corpse of Jane Harlow, its back bent and arms dangling like an ape. Clint turned to the second attacker. At least this one looked like a human being.

"Killed a couple of my buddies back there, you bastard," the man told Clint. "Gonna enjoy watchin' you squirm with a bolt in your belly, feller."

He was about average height and build with tawny hair and a collection of peach fuzz on his jaw and upper lip. He wore Levi's and a blue denim work shirt and carried a six-gun on his hip, although he held a crossbow ready in his hands. A vicious smile slithered across his youthful face.

"Wanna start beggin' before or after I stick you with this thing?" he asked.

Clint Adams merely glared back at him, breathing deeply through his nose and out his mouth, trying to clear his head enough to make his move.

"Suit yourself, feller." The killer shrugged as he aimed the crossbow at Clint.

The Gunsmith suddenly rolled to the left. The crossbow fired its missile. The bolt struck the ground where Clint had been a moment before, the shaft waving its feathered end like a miniature flag.

"Shit," the killer growled, reaching for his sidearm.

Clint's hand dove to the bundle of clothing. He clawed at the small .22-caliber New Line Colt and swiftly raised it, pointing the muzzle at his opponent's lower torso.

"Oh, Christ!" the man exclaimed in astonishment and terror.

"You'll get to meet Him in person," the Gunsmith hissed as he squeezed the trigger.

A .22 round tore into the man's lower intestines. He screamed and clawed at the gun on his hip. Clint fired the New Line again, drilling a bullet through the killer's right forearm. The man's hand flew away from his holster, blood splattering the sleeve of his shirt.

Clint glanced around quickly, searching for the primitive man which had accompanied the hootowl. Yet, just like the apparition of evil it resembled, the creature had vanished.

The Gunsmith located his .45 Colt and quickly scooped it up. He scanned the forest for some sign of the other man. *Bolo*, he thought. *The other guy had called him Bolo. And Jane had said Bolo wasn't human. . . .*

Maybe she was right.

Whatever Bolo was, he had obviously managed to flee into the forest. Clint stared at the trees, ignoring the suffering cries of the wounded man on the ground. The bastard had killed Jane. Let him suffer for a while.

Jane.

Clint glanced at the ground where her body had been. She was gone. Bolo had carried her off when he escaped. The Gunsmith debated whether or not to try to hunt down the big savage. Stalking a creature like that in a dark forest didn't appeal to Clint Adams.

"Finish me!" the injured gunman pleaded. "Oh, God! For the love of Christ, finish me!"

"You would have left me to die in agony if things had turned out different," the Gunsmith snapped.

"No, I wouldn't," the man sobbed. "Please . . ."

"You're lying, fella," Clint told him as he approached

the wounded man. "You'd have stood by and laughed as I died. There'd be no merciful bullet from you if I was in your place right now."

"Please, mister . . ."

The Gunsmith quickly aimed his .45 at the man's skull and squeezed the trigger. The echo of the gunshot filled the forest, but the man's cries for mercy ceased.

"But I'm not you," Clint told the corpse at his feet. "Thank God for that."

TEN

Clint Adams wearily glanced about at the simple wood and brick structures that comprised the community of Eagle's Gap. It resembled a hundred other towns Clint had seen in a dozen different states.

The Gunsmith barely glanced at the local saloon although two whores stood at the batwings and called out invitations for him to join them inside. Clint made note of the locations of the livery stable and the McCrae Hotel in case he decided to stay in Eagle's Gap after paying the sheriff a visit.

Clint stopped his rig at the local law office. A tall, slender figure emerged from the building as Clint climbed down from his wagon. The tin star pinned on the man's vest told of his occupation and a hard-eyed, tight-lipped expression warned Clint that the lawman wasn't in a very good mood.

"Morning, Sheriff," the Gunsmith greeted. He figured such an uncomplicated remark wouldn't be apt to upset the already perturbed lawman.

"Howdy," the sheriff replied curtly.

"Could I talk to you for a few minutes?" Clint asked. "It's important."

"I ain't goin' nowhere for a while, son," the lawman answered.

"Uh-huh," Clint muttered. "My name is Clint—"

"I know who you are, son," the sheriff interrupted. "You're Clint Adams and you're better known as the Gunsmith. When I saw that big black horse tied to the back of your rig, I figured who you must be. Then I seen that scar on your cheek and I knew for positive."

"You've got a keen eye, Sheriff," the Gunsmith remarked.

"Name's Cooper," the lawman told him. "Don't imagine you've heard of me since I ain't famous like'n you are."

"Fame isn't all it's cracked up to be," Clint said. "At least it hasn't been so great from my point of view."

"Yeah," Cooper commented. "Reckon it is sorta tiresome havin' to fret 'bout gunhawks hungry for a reputation."

"Real tiresome." Clint nodded.

"Heard tell that you wander from town to town workin' as a for-real gunsmith," Cooper said. "Ain't never heard of you startin' trouble, so I reckon no one will mind if'n you stay in town for a spell . . . so long as you don't litter up Eagle's Gap with dead bodies."

"I appreciate that, Sheriff," Clint replied. "But I've actually come to talk to you about some things that have been happening recently around this area."

"What sort of things, son?"

"Sheriff, I don't think you and I are kin to each other." Clint sighed. "And you can't be more than five or six years older than me, so don't call me son unless you know something I don't."

Cooper shrugged. "What sort of things, feller?"

"Four killings for a start," the Gunsmith answered. "I had to kill three men in self-defense. Buried two of them back in the forest somewhere between here and Wido.

EAGLE'S GAP 57

About twelve miles west of here. The fourth killing was
the murder of a girl who used to live in this town—Jane
Harlow. The fella who killed her also tried to murder me,
but I got him instead. He's lying in the back of my wagon
if you care to take a—''

"Hell, feller." Cooper whistled softly. "You say this
is what you got to *start* with?''

"I'm not sure you'll believe the rest of it.''

"Reckon we can talk this over with some coffee?'' the
sheriff asked. "Got some brewin' in my office, if'n you
figure that'd be to your taste, Mr. Adams.''

"Just call me Clint,'' the Gunsmith urged. "And your
offer sounds right generous, Sheriff. Thanks.''

Sheriff Cooper had an unusual recipe for good coffee.
He added two spoons of brown sugar to each cup and then
poured in half a shot of red-eye. Clint wondered how often
the lawman consumed his "Irish coffee.'' If he made a
frequent habit of it, Cooper would be ready to trade in his
badge for a broom in a couple years. The change from
lawman to a town drunk who sweeps out saloons and
stables had happened to more than one man when he got
too fond of the bottle.

Clint had seen how liquor had whittled down Bill
Hickok and he'd had a bout with alcohol himself following his old friend's death. The Gunsmith knew he had to
watch how much he drank and he generally restricted
himself to two drinks at one sitting. However, he found
himself wanting more whiskey-laced coffee.

And he knew why.

Jane Harlow's face was still vividly engraved in his
memory. He had known her for only a few hours, yet he
had heard the story of her life and her broken dreams of
fame as a circus performer. He'd made love to her under

the stars and seen her die right in front of him.

Clint could still see her face, contorted by pain and pleading for help. Jane had trusted him to protect her from Feltrinelli's hired killers. The Gunsmith's stomach knotted when he recalled how casually he'd dismissed the danger and promised her that everything would be all right. And she'd believed him, openly giving her body although many men had forced themselves on her in the past.

That had been careless. Stupid and careless. Coupling naked right out in the open while the enemy was closing in for the kill. The famous Gunsmith who was greased lightning with a six-gun and the veteran of dozens of battles with the toughest hombres in the West—bullshit. He'd stood naked with his fabled double-action Colt in his fist while the bastards murdered Jane Harlow.

Some things aren't easy for a man to live with. Clint knew that this was one memory he'd have a tough time getting under control. The only way he knew of to do that was to see to it Feltrinelli paid for his crimes.

"Care for another cup of coffee, Clint?" Cooper asked, holding the tin pot in one hand and the red-eye bottle in the other.

"No thanks," he replied. "I think I've had enough. Well, Sheriff, I've told you what happened. Now, what do we do about it?"

"Clint," the lawman said wearily, "I don't rightly know what can be done. Mind you, I ain't callin' you a liar or nothin' like that, but that's a mighty tall tale you spun. Kinda hard to believe without some solid evidence."

"I've got some evidence lying stiff as an oakwood board. Evidence with three bullets in him that's stinking up my wagon."

"A dead man doesn't prove a goddamn circus is involved in these wild crimes you're claiming have occurred," Cooper replied.

"What about those crossbows?" Clint asked. "I've got two crossbows with extra bolts for each of them. Where do you figure I picked those up?"

"I don't claim to know much about such contraptions," the sheriff began. "But wouldn't it be mighty easy for a professional gunsmith, like yourself, to make those crossbows? Gotta be easier than modifying a single-action Colt forty-five to fire double-action, right?"

"But I *didn't* make them," Clint insisted.

"I believe you, Clint," the lawman said hastily. "But will a court of law? You know this Feltrinelli is a shrewd feller. Bound to get hisself a smart lawyer. You were a lawman yourself long enough to know how these things work."

"What about Jane Harlow?" the Gunsmith demanded. "How do you explain the fact that I knew about her?"

"You don't have to convince me, Clint," Cooper assured him. "But you don't have any proof about the girl. No body, no clothes—nothing."

"But how could I even know she existed?" Clint insisted.

"Everybody around these parts knew that Jane had gone and joined a circus," Cooper answered. "An attorney might say you could have overheard the story in a saloon and just sort of added onto it."

"For what reason?"

"I don't know." Cooper shrugged. "Maybe a lawyer would suggest you were trying to come up with some sort of explanation for how that bank in Wido was robbed."

"How else could the thieves have robbed that bank under those circumstances if Feltrinelli didn't do it?"

"A balloon full of acrobats flying into a town in the

middle of the night sounds pretty farfetched, Clint.'' The sheriff gave an apologetic shrug. ''Sort of like something a feller might dream up who has a reputation for solving unusual crimes after every other answer had him stumped.''

''You're right,'' Clint admitted. ''A clever lawyer could make my story look absurd—especially one as clever as you.''

''Shit.'' Cooper sniffled. ''I ain't even had no proper schooling. I just read a lot. Got a couple law books I've read four or five times, that's all.''

The Gunsmith realized there was more to Sheriff Cooper than met the eye. He wasn't the surly, narrow-minded, uneducated small-town lawman he first appeared to be. Clint wondered how Cooper wound up in a place like Eagle's Gap. Yet, had he accomplished more with his life than the sheriff?

The hell with it, he decided. *Every man is different. Doesn't make any sense to make comparisons.*

''Sounds like I'll just have to get some more evidence.'' The Gunsmith shrugged.

''Hold on, Clint,'' Cooper began. ''I don't know what you're thinking, but you'd best not have any vigilante notions in your head.''

''Right now,'' Clint said, ''I'd just like to have a talk with Martha Harlow, Jane's sister. How about telling me where I can find her.''

''Just a minute, Clint,'' Cooper said. ''You've got a dead body in your wagon. We have to do something about that.''

''How about burying the son of a bitch?'' Clint suggested. ''I sure as hell don't want to keep him.''

''Well . . .'' Cooper began.

''Sheriff!'' an excited voice cried.

Both men turned to see the wiry red-haired youth who had just burst through the door. Although he didn't wear a gun, the badge pinned to his shirt revealed he was Cooper's deputy.

"There's a corpse in the back of that wagon outside," he declared.

"I know, Merv. Mr. Adams here brought the feller in. I'm trying to figure out what we should do about it."

"Have you taken a look at that body yet, Sheriff?" Merv asked.

"I've seen dead men before."

"Ever see a dead Duran?" the deputy remarked. " 'Cause that's what's lyin' in that wagon."

"Duran?" Cooper rose from his chair with a start. "Which one?"

"Luke, the youngest," Merv replied. "Matthew and Mark ain't gonna take news of this very peaceable, Sheriff."

"The Duran brothers come from West Virginia," Cooper told Clint. "Their daddy was a Baptist preacher full of righteous anger, fire and brimstone. Named his sons Matthew, Mark and Luke after the first three books of the New Testament. Probably figured to have himself a fourth son and name him John, but the preacher's wife ran out on him."

"The old man was mighty strict with his boys," Merv added. "Maybe that's why they sort of went wild after the preacher died."

"The Durans are uncouth, superstitious misfits," the sheriff explained. "And they've got an Old Testament sense of justice."

"And you know what it says in the Book of Numbers, chapter thirty-five, verse nineteen," Merv said. " 'The avenger of blood shall himself put the murderer to death;

when he meets him, he shall put him to death.' ''

"I'd be grateful if you'd move on as soon as possible, Clint," Cooper admitted. "Just as soon not have a show-down between you and the Duran brothers in my town."

"I don't want that either," the Gunsmith assured him. "But I still have to talk to Martha Harlow."

ELEVEN

The Harlow dairy farm was located two miles north of
Eagle's Gap. Clint Adams had no trouble finding the
place. The farm was small, consisting of a house, a
windmill and a barn with a tiny pasture where two cows
and a bull were grazing.

The Gunsmith urged Duke forward and rode to the
house. He dismounted and prepared to walk to the porch,
but he heard someone moving in the barn. Clint recognized the sound of a woman breathing heavily from exer-
tion.

"Hope I'm not about to interrupt something personal,"
he muttered as he headed toward the sound.

A large white sign with red letters was posted by the
door of the barn. It read: MILK IS THE MOST WHOLESOME OF
FOODS. A smaller sign bore the legend: SWEET DREAMS ARE
MADE OF CHEESE.

"Who am I to disagree?" Clint whispered with a shrug.

The sound of the woman's labored breathing steered
Clint around the barn to the east side. He peered around
the corner, half expecting to see a woman indulged in
sexual activity with her husband or sweetheart. He sure as
hell didn't expect to see what was actually in progress.

A young woman, clad in Levi trousers and a man's
work shirt, was swinging from a horizontal bar mounted

on a pair of wooden supports. She agilely sailed from the bar to another positioned nearby. Seizing the second bar, the girl's body whipped clear around it, whirling like a top.

Then she released the bar, twisted in midair and caught it again to launch herself at the first bar. She seized the bar and began to execute another series of gymnastic revolutions when she saw Clint Adams.

"Oh," the girl said breathlessly. "Howdy, mister."

"Good afternoon," the Gunsmith replied. "Sorry to disturb you, ma'am."

She suddenly hauled herself onto the bar, placing her midsection across it. The girl spun over the bar and landed feet first on the ground. She threw back her head to swing her long black hair, fashioned in a single braid, away from her face.

"What can I do for you, mister?" she asked as she approached.

"Are you Martha Harlow?" Clint inquired.

"That's right," she answered. "And somehow I don't think you came here to buy some milk or cheese."

The girl certainly didn't resemble Jane Harlow. She was taller, at least five years older, with jet black hair and dark brown eyes. However, she had the same long, lean, incredibly fit body and limbs and her cheekbones were high above a wide, full mouth.

"I've got some news for you," Clint began, his chest constricting as if an internal fist had suddenly gripped his heart. "About your sister."

"Janie?" Martha raised her eyebrows. "Did something happen to her?"

"Well, I was traveling in my wagon from Wido when I saw her come out of the forest . . ."

"What happened to her?" Martha demanded.

"She's dead, ma'am," Clint said softly. "I'm sorry."

"Oh, my God," the girl whispered in disbelief. "Janie can't be dead. She's only eighteen years old . . ."

"I'm sorry," the Gunsmith repeated, unable to think of anything else to say.

"She got a job with a circus." Martha shook her head, tears streaming down her cheeks. "But she said it wasn't dangerous. I should have known better. Janie was always a headstrong kid. Did she miss the net or bounce out and land off balance on the ground?"

"Your sister's death wasn't an accident," Clint told her bluntly. "She was murdered."

"Murdered?" Martha glared at him. "That's—Why would anyone want to kill Janie?"

"I think I'd better explain this whole thing from the beginning."

"You can start by telling me just who the hell you are, mister!" Martha snapped, wiping a hand across her moist eyes. "I mean, a goddamn stranger comes out of nowhere and tells me my sister is—"

"I'm the man who's going to find the man who ordered the murder of your sister," the Gunsmith replied in a hard flat voice. "And when I do, I'm going to nail his balls to a tree before I kill him."

Martha stared at Clint. She saw something few people had ever witnessed and lived to tell about. The Gunsmith's eyes were clouded with cold, deadly anger. The fury was enormous, yet completely under the man's control. It was a force, raw energy that could be unleashed with devastating potential like a tornado harnessed and transformed into human form.

"I've got some blackberry wine in the house," Martha said. "Maybe we should have a glass or two while you tell me what happened, Mr. . . . ?"

"Adams. Clint Adams."

"You're the Gunsmith?" she gasped.

"That's what some folks call me, ma'am," he admitted.

Clint told Martha his tale as they sat in her kitchen, sipping blackberry wine. The girl stared into her glass and listened to the conclusion of his story.

"And you're sure there isn't enough proof to have this Feltrinelli character arrested?" Martha asked.

"Maybe." Clint shrugged. "But the odds of having him found guilty in a court of law wouldn't be very good. I'm going to have to get some more evidence about the Circus Incredible."

"How?"

"First I'm going to find the damn circus," the Gunsmith explained. "That shouldn't be too difficult. Then I'll try to figure out how to handle the problem after I've actually seen what I'm up against."

"But the savage who attacked you with the boomerang saw you—" Martha began.

"A boomerang?" Clint raised his eyebrows.

"From the description, I'd say that was the curved stick he threw at you which traveled in a wide arch and then sailed straight at your skull," Martha answered. "A boomerang is designed to be thrown in a circle at its target. It'll even swing back to its owner if it misses so he can try to throw it again."

"Jesus," Clint whispered. "How'd you know about that?"

"My father was Australian," the girl said. "He was a magician with a carnival down under. He told us about the aborigines in the outback. They're primitive, but very clever and highly skilled at hunting and tracking in a manner that seems to defy the laws of logic."

"Then Bolo is one of these Australian aborigines?" Clint mused.

"He sure sounds like it," Martha confirmed. "Father said they looked like creatures from another time."

"Why did he have all those scars crisscrossing his face?"

"Tribal custom maybe. Part of a religious sect or a hunting tattoo that's supposed to protect him from evil spirits. It's hard to say."

"Do you think Jane was right? Can Bolo actually track by scent like a bloodhound?"

"Father claimed that he saw outback natives do exactly that," she replied. "And the boomerang is pretty positive evidence that Bolo is just such an aborigine."

"Well, a throwing stick is no match for a Colt forty-five," Clint declared. "Next time I see that son of a bitch, I'll put a bullet up his nose. See how well he smells people out after that."

"You can't just charge into the circus with six-guns blazing," Martha said. "We'll have to make some sort of plan."

"*We?*" Clint frowned. "You're not thinking of coming with me, are you?"

"I most certainly *am.*"

"Absolutely not," he told her.

"They killed my sister and carried off her body so she won't even get a decent funeral and you think I'm just going to sit here and wait for you to come back and tell me what happened? Not this girl."

"These people are dangerous," Clint insisted. "They've already killed four people . . . probably a lot of others we don't know about as well."

"And one of them was Janie," Martha said firmly. "I'm going with you."

"No you're not," he said sharply. "I've already got the burden of your sister's death on my conscience. I don't want to take the chance that you'll get killed too."

"My life is my concern," she told him. "Not yours. If I don't leave with you, I'll go after them on my own."

"Aw, hell," Clint growled, well aware the girl meant what she said. "Okay, but I want you to promise that you won't try anything rash. When we catch up with the circus, I'm in charge of how we handle Feltrinelli and his crew. If I give you an order, you'll do what I say. Agreed?"

"Agreed." She nodded.

"I bet," Clint muttered sourly. "A hardheaded woman like you isn't the sort to take to being bossed by any man."

"But I'll listen to someone with your experience in matters I know little about," Martha assured him. "Don't worry. I'll listen to you. Promise."

"What about your farm?"

"I can get some friends to look after the place while I'm gone."

"All right." The Gunsmith sighed. "I just hope you know what you're getting yourself into."

"I do," she said firmly.

"Fine." Clint smiled. "Maybe you ought to tell me because I don't really know what to expect from a bunch of hootowls with a bag of deadly tricks like the Circus Incredible seems to have."

"I guess that's something we'll find out together."

TWELVE

Martha fixed dinner for her guest. Clint hadn't paid his appetite much mind since the night before when he saw Jane Harlow die. He was surprised when the scent of steaks, potatoes and corn on the cob abruptly revived his hunger. The Gunsmith had a hearty meal. Martha, still depressed by the recent news of her sister's death, ate little.

"You probably noticed that Janie didn't look much like me," Martha remarked. "She was actually my aunt's daughter, but we raised her since she was a baby. You see, my aunt didn't think it was a good idea to bring up a child because she wasn't married when she gave birth to Janie."

Martha stared at a wall without seeing it as she spoke. "We were the only family Janie ever knew. She was never told who her real mother was."

"Would it have mattered?" Clint remarked. "Family are the people who raise you and love you. Isn't that what really matters?"

"I wouldn't have thought a man with your reputation as a gunfighter would be so understanding," Martha said. I don't mean to offend you—"

"That's okay," Clint assured her. "I do have a reputation, but I never wanted it. Don't believe everything you read in the newspapers. A lot of two-legged maggots write quite a bit of what winds up in print. It's true I've been in some gunfights and I've killed a few men, but that doesn't mean I'm incapable of human emotions.''

Martha smiled. ''I'm glad you were the one who was with Janie before she died.''

''I just stood there and watched,'' the Gunsmith said bitterly.

''What could you have done?'' Martha placed a hand on Clint's shoulder. ''I'm glad you're here with me now and that we'll be stalking Janie's killers together.''

''That reminds me,'' Clint said. ''We should head after them as soon as possible. The circus must be close by right now, but the longer we wait the more time they'll have to put more miles between them and us.''

''I'll talk to my friends about looking after the farm tomorrow morning. I should be ready to leave by noon.''

''All I have to do is get my wagon out of the livery back at Eagle's Gap,'' Clint said. ''I can do that tonight and camp in the woods near your property.''

''Hal Davis owns the livery,'' Martha explained. ''He closes the place at exactly eight-thirty every night and doesn't open it until dawn.''

''A mighty poor businessman,'' Clint muttered. ''What if somebody arrives in town late at night?''

''That's their problem, not Hal's.''

''Great,'' he growled. ''Well, can I sleep in the barn tonight?''

Martha opened her mouth to say something. Whatever it was, she obviously reconsidered it and said, ''Sure. I'll get you some blankets.''

''There's a bedroll on my saddle,'' Clint told her. ''I'll be fine. . . .''

The sound of hooves striking the ground caught their

attention. Martha rose from her chair and headed for the door. Clint followed, automatically releasing the thong from the hammer of his Colt. The girl peered out a window.

"It's the sheriff," she said, opening the door.

"Howdy, Miss Harlow," Cooper's voice greeted. "Sorry to disturb you, but I wondered if'n a feller named Clint Adams is still visiting you."

"Yes, he is, Sheriff," Martha answered. "He came to tell me about my sister."

"I know, ma'am," Cooper said as he swung down from the back of his horse. "But I gotta tell Clint something that I reckon he'd best know about."

"I'm right here, Sheriff," the Gunsmith announced, stepping onto the porch.

"You recall me warning you about the Duran brothers?" the sheriff began. "Well, Matthew and Mark Duran jumped my deputy while he was making his rounds. They beat the shit—pardon my language, ma'am—they beat him up and made him tell who killed their kid brother."

"Did he mention that I might be here to tell Martha what happened?" Clint asked.

"Ain't sure if Merv told 'em that or not," Cooper replied. "He ain't real sure himself. Anyway, they left town after working over Merv and I don't know where the polecats might'a run to."

"I'd better go back to town with you, Sheriff," the Gunsmith said. "I don't want to endanger Martha by staying in her barn tonight."

"But if you ride back with the sheriff you'll both be vulnerable to an ambush," Martha stated. "They'll have the advantage in the dark."

"You got a point there, Miss Harlow," Cooper agreed. "And they'd kill me as well as Clint. After what they've already done tonight, they know they won't be able to head back home like nothin' ever happened.''

"And if they do show up here,'' Martha continued, "I'd rather Clint was close by to protect me.''

"Well, Clint?'' the sheriff asked. "Reckon it's up to you.''

"Everybody seems to think I should stay.'' The Gunsmith shrugged. "So I guess I'll go along with the idea.''

"Take care,'' Cooper warned as he climbed onto his horse. "Those Duran brothers are plumb loco and they're out for your blood.''

THIRTEEN

Clint Adams crinkled his nose when he smelled the strong odor of manure in the barn. Several cows looked toward him with disinterested eyes. None of them even uttered a moo, content to chew their cuds in peace.

The Gunsmith had never had much to do with cattle of any kind and he knew little about them except they were dumber than horses and they tasted good after they'd been cut up and cooked. He thought the smaller fawn-colored cows were Jerseys and he recognized the Herefords only because they had distinct white faces. Clint was about as interested in the cows as they appeared to be in him.

"There you are, big fella," Clint remarked when he approached Duke's stall. "You doing okay in here with all these females?"

Duke snorted in reply.

"Don't fret," Clint said, stroking the gelding's neck. "We'll be leaving in the morning. Right now, I'm going to get my bedroll and—"

"Don't push me!" Martha's voice snapped.

She'd spoken loudly enough for the Gunsmith to hear her, which was probably what she intended. The girl wasn't alone. Clint immediately lifted the globe of his lantern and blew out the flame. He placed it on the floorboards, clear of any flammable materials and drew his Colt.

The Gunsmith quickly moved to a stack of bails of hay and slipped behind them. He peered around the edge, exposing only his right eye, and waited for the barn door to open. Less than five seconds later, it did.

Two men, a tall slender blond and a stocky dark-haired fellow, entered. The blond held Martha, one arm wrapped around her throat from behind with the muzzle of a pistol jammed against the side of her head. The dark-headed man raised a lantern high, his left hand fisted around the bail while his right held a six-gun.

"Could'a swore I seen some light afore we headed this way, Matthew," he remarked as he scanned the interior of the barn.

" 'Course we did, Mark," the blond replied. "The bastard must'a heard this bitch warn him. The coward is hidin' on us."

Matthew and Mark, Clint thought, recalling the names of the Duran brothers. He aimed his Colt at the tow-headed Matthew, his finger ready on the trigger. The Gunsmith held his fire, Martha was too close.

"Clint Adams!" Mark shouted. "We know you be hidin' in here. Come on out, boy. Ain't no place you can run to."

"Adams!" Matthew added. "If'n you don't come out, I'm gonna have to kill this pretty gal. Don't want me to blow her head off, do you?"

"We gotta score to settle with you, Adams," Mark declared. "Ain't no reason to get the girl killed too. We'll find you anyway. Eye for an eye, tooth for a tooth, like it says in the Good Book. Reckon it applies to a life for a life when somebody done murdered your brother."

"Ain't gonna make it hard for you, Adams," Matthew declared. "Luke weren't real close to us. Wouldn't mind us worth a darn. Tried to whup some sense into that boy, but he never had no respect for his elders.''

"Run off about five or six months ago," Mark said as he moved farther into the barn. "We figured we was finally shed of him. Almost a blessin', what with him being such a natural-born sinner and all.''

"So you see," Matthew began, dragging Martha as he followed his brother, "We ain't plannin' on draggin' out your execution. We'll be quick and merciful.''

"I still don't see the son of a bitch," Mark muttered. "Maybe he sneaked out another door or somethin'.''

"There's no one in here," Martha told her captors. "I already explained to you two that Clint Adams rode out here, told me about my sister's death and rode on back to home.''

"Can't rightly believe that, ma'am," Matthew said. "Mark and me bein' watchin' the road for some time. Seen the sheriff ride out here, but he rode back alone.''

"Yeah," Mark added. "And I see a big black hoss over yonder. Heard tell this Gunsmith feller has hisself a critter like that.''

"Best come out now, Adams," Matthew warned. "We're apt to get plenty mean if'n you make us wait on you. Might even decide to cut up this gal to convince you to show yourself.''

The front sight of Clint's Colt bisected Matthew Duran's face as he gazed down the barrel of his revolver. A perfect head shot, yet Clint held his fire. Even if he put a bullet through the man's brain, Matthew could still shoot Martha if a muscle reflex triggered his weapon.

"I know where Adams is," a high-pitched, reedy voice declared.

The Gunsmith stiffened, startled by the statement and

totally baffled as to who had spoken. Matthew Duran asked the same question that was on Clint's mind at the moment.

"Who said that?" the gunman demanded.

"Didn't the gal say it?" Mark Duran asked.

"Shit," Matthew replied. "I've got the bitch right here with me. I'd know if she said somethin', wouldn't I?"

"Then who said it?" Mark asked.

"That's what I already said, you moron," Matthew growled. "Whoever it is, the voice came from that stall over yonder."

"Reckon it's Adams tryin' to disguise his voice to catch us off guard somehow?" Mark inquired, swinging his gun toward the stall.

"Go find out," Matthew instructed. "But be careful."

"It wasn't Clint," Martha said, twisting her head away, but Matthew kept the gun pressed against her skull.

"Then who is it?" he demanded.

"You won't believe me," she replied.

"I'm right here," the reedy voice declared. "Don't be afraid. I won't hurt you."

"Just come on out with your hands up," Mark began as he approached the stall, his pistol held ready.

"Can't," the voice said. "I don't have any hands."

"What the hell is this crap?" Matthew muttered.

"I'm comin' in after you," Mark warned as he entered the stall.

The Gunsmith was as confused as the Duran brothers. He didn't know where the voice was coming from, but it was drawing the gunmen away from his position. He continued to wait for a clear target . . . and wondered what the hell was going on.

"Mark!" Matthew snapped. "You find anybody in there?"

"Ain't nobody in this stall 'cept for a cow," the younger Duran brother replied.

"Don't be stupid," Matthew said. "Check that stall out careful like. Look under the cow too. Must be a kid in there or somethin'."

"There ain't, Matt," Mark insisted. "There's just this damn cow a chewin' its cud."

"And just who do you think has been talking to you, young man?" the reedy voice inquired.

"Sweet Jesus on Palm Sunday!" Mark exclaimed.

"You find the kid, Mark?" Matthew asked.

"Ain't no kid," the younger man replied. "The cow said it!"

"What the hell are you talking about?"

"Matt, there ain't nobody else here!" Mark insisted.

"You been sneakin' drinks outta the corn liquor jug again?" Matthew accused.

"I tell you this here cow musta said it, Matt," his brother declared.

"I told you you wouldn't believe it." Martha shrugged.

"Cows can't talk." Matthew rolled his eyes. "I never heard me such bullshit."

"Hold on, Matt," Mark began. "There was a talking donkey mentioned in the Bible. Don't you remember Onan's mule?"

"Onan didn't have no talkin' mule," Matthew replied. "The Lord smote him dead for lopin' his mule and spillin' his seed on the ground."

"Well, *somebody* had a talkin' jackass," Mark insisted.

"I got one for a brother."

"If Matt doesn't want to believe I can talk," the reedy voice remarked, "then I just won't talk to him."

"Did you hear that?" Mark demanded, staring at the

small Jersey cow in the stall. "Did you see her lips move when she spoke?"

"Cow's just chewin' its cud," Matthew said, but he moved closer for a better look. "Ain't it?"

"Do you two want to know where Adams is hiding?" the voice inquired.

"That's right, cow." Mark nodded.

"Then you let Martha go," the animal seemed to say. "She feeds me and cares for me and keeps my secret."

"We won't hurt her," Mark promised. "Will we, Matt?"

"Er . . . no," the older Duran assured the cow. "We just want Adams is all."

"You've offended me." The cow looked up at Matthew as its mouth churned methodically. "Why should I tell you where Adams is? You're both impolite."

"Don't say that," Mark urged, patting the animal's neck. "We're really nice fellers. Come on, now. Where's Adams?"

"Ask me nice," the voice insisted.

"Please," Matthew began awkwardly. "Please tell me, cow . . ."

"That's better," the cow seemed to say. "Adams sneaked out a loose board in the wall. He's probably waiting for you outside."

"I'll be go to hell," Matthew whispered, lowering his revolver from Martha's skull.

The Gunsmith's .45 roared. A tongue of orange flame streaked from the bails of hay and Matthew Duran's head snapped backward as a bullet burned a merciless path through his brain.

Mark Duran whirled and fired at the muzzle flash of Clint's gun. Hay spat from the bails. Cows mooed mournfully. Duran cocked the hammer of his revolver for another shot, but Clint Adams triggered his double-action Colt twice before his opponent could open fire.

Mark Duran received two 230-grain bullets through the heart. His body fell across the chest of his dead brother who already lay sprawled across the floor near the stall of the "talking cow." The Gunsmith emerged from his hiding place, the smoking Colt pistol still in his fist.

"You okay, Martha?" he asked.

"I'm fine," she assured him. "Thanks to you and Josie here."

Martha patted the cow's head. The animal calmly continued to chew its cud. The Gunsmith looked at the cow suspiciously.

"Okay," he began. "How'd you do it?"

"A little trick my father taught me." Martha smiled. "I told you he was a magician, remember?"

"Ventriloquism." Clint grinned.

"Right." The girl glanced down at the Duran brothers. "And it sure worked on those two dummies."

FOURTEEN

"I'm going to run out of blackberry wine at this rate," Martha Harlow declared as she poured two glasses of the rich dark liquid for herself and Clint Adams.

"I was impressed by how you handled that situation," the Gunsmith told her as he sat at the table in her kitchen.

"Oh, I'm not really a very good ventriloquist," she said. "My father would have convinced those two that the barn was haunted. They would have been hearing voices from the floors and ceiling and everywhere else."

"Well, you seemed to do well enough," Clint assured her. "But what really impressed me was how you kept your head. You can think clearly under pressure. You did just fine."

"I was terrified," Martha admitted.

"Of course you were," Clint said. "You'd be a damn fool if you weren't scared when a man had a gun pressed against your head. What makes a difference is whether you freeze up under that sort of a situation. You didn't."

"I still don't want to spend the night alone," the girl told him.

The Gunsmith's eyes traveled from her lovely face to the tempting display of cleavage at the V-shaped front of her robe. Clint's manhood began to stir with expectation, but he warned himself not to jump to conclusions.

"I can set up my bedroll here on the kitchen floor," he said.

"That won't be necessary," Martha said, looking down at her glass. "There's a bed."

Clint rose from his chair and moved to her side. Martha lifted her face, eyes closed, lips parted to invite a kiss. His lips met hers and their mouths pressed together hard, tongues exploring eagerly.

Martha rose from her chair as well, climbing into the Gunsmith's embrace. She caught Clint's tongue in her teeth and gently chewed it as his hands moved to the front of her robe. He unfastened the cloth belt and peeled the garment from her shoulders. The robe fell in a heap at her ankles.

Her body was superb. Martha's breasts were small and perfectly formed. Her trim waist extended to narrow hips and long, beautiful legs with sleek firm muscles. Martha took his hand.

"Let me show you the bedroom," she whispered.

Martha led Clint from the kitchen to the next room. A large four-poster bed with a quilt covering the mattress waited for them. He quickly unbuckled his gunbelt and hung it over the post at the head of the bed.

"You always keep that gun close by?" she asked.

"I have to," Clint replied as he unbuttoned his shirt. "I'll have to for the rest of my life."

"I understand," Martha assured him as she moved closer.

The girl reached down to stroke the bulge at his crotch, then began to unbutton his fly. The Gunsmith almost ripped his shirt off, his passion burning within him like a range fire.

Martha pulled down Clint's pants. She took his swollen cock in her mouth, rolling her tongue around the stiff fleshy shaft. Martha drew on him gently, moving her lips up and down the length of his penis from root to head. She cupped his balls in her hand, fingertips massaging the sensitive sack as she skillfully sucked his manhood.

"Martha," Clint whispered. "I'm getting near the brink."

She responded by sucking him harder, her head moving back and forth faster and faster. At last, she drew Clint's seed from him. The Gunsmith groaned with pleasure as his load exploded into her mouth. The girl continued to suck, milking his cock until he figured his testicles would be flat.

"Jesus," Clint gasped as she finished.

Martha rose, smiled at Clint and lay back on the bed. The Gunsmith joined her, his hands stroking her warm smooth flesh. He found her breasts and fondled them, thumbing the brown-tipped nipples erect. Clint kissed and sucked them as he moved his fingers to the girl's thighs.

"That's it, Clint," Martha whispered. "Oh, that feels good."

The Gunsmith's tongue traveled down Martha's flat belly. He licked a circle slowly around the rim of her navel before moving his mouth lower. The musky scent of her womanhood filled Clint's nostrils as he sunk his tongue inside her.

"Oh, God!" Martha gasped.

Clint lunged his tongue deeper, rolling it inside her love center. Martha convulsed, groaning as the Gunsmith lapped faster and faster. The girl's legs embraced his shoulders, her thighs hugging his head firmly as she trembled in the joy of an orgasm.

"Oh, that was wonderful," Martha sighed.

Clint continued to stroke the girl, taking his time, fondling and kissing, probing and stroking, gradually bringing her to a frenzy of passion.

Martha seized Clint's penis and almost desperately pulled it inside of her. The Gunsmith still didn't rush, working himself deeper at a steady pace until he felt her body buck and thrash eagerly. Then he rammed home faster and faster until they both rode to glory in unison.

"Clint Adams," the girl said breathlessly, "you are one helluva man."

The Gunsmith kissed her gently and ran his fingers through her long black hair. Then he proceeded to confirm her evaluation of him as they began to make love once more.

FIFTEEN

The Gunsmith and Martha Harlow left the following afternoon, traveling together in Clint's wagon with Duke attached to a guideline at the rear of the rig. For three days and nights they were on the trail, camping after sundown and making love under the stars.

On the fourth day they approached a small town called Brady. Less than a quarter of a mile to the west of the town was a huge canvas tent surrounded by an assortment of wagons and cages on wheels. Above the big top, undeniable proof that they had found the right circus, floated a hot air balloon.

The Gunsmith had seen such airships before and they had never failed to impress him. "Aerostatic machines" had been invented in France back in 1783. Hot air balloons had improved a lot since then. There had even been an Army Aeronautic Section during the War Between the States, headed by Thaddeus Sobieski Coulincourt Lowe who used balloons to observe the activities of Confederate forces which he then reported to the Union Army.

Clint had always found the idea of men actually flying to be fascinating; he'd never considered an aerostat as a sinister device . . . until that very moment.

The balloon was jet black. The spherical bag was connected to an ebony basket by black load cables. Clint realized he was looking at the same device that had been used to float thieves into Wido in the dead of night. *The Black Moon*, Jane Harlow had called it. The name suited the balloon which seemed to be almost a supernatural vehicle of evil as it hovered silently in the sky, a black shadowy predator waiting to swoop down and strike.

"We've found them, Clint," Martha declared in a tense whisper. She was also staring up at the balloon with awe and apprehension.

"I noticed," the Gunsmith remarked. "Now we just have to figure out what we're going to do about it."

"We've already discussed that," Martha said.

"I know." Clint nodded. "But I can't say I'm exactly thrilled with the plan we came up with. It's too risky."

"You're worried about me?" She smiled.

"Yeah," he admitted. "Let's get a better look at the setup and decide what we'll do then."

As they rode through the streets of Brady, the couple saw the balloon more vividly. It was attached to a pair of long cables which kept the craft in fixed flight. Four men held the guidelines below. Clint counted four passengers in the basket. He tried to guess how high above ground the balloon was floating. At least two hundred feet, he reckoned.

The men at the lines began to pull the cables. Others assisted them and gradually they began to lower the balloon. When the vessel touched down, the roustabouts grabbed the hoop of the basket to hold it down. Three of the passengers climbed out and another trio took their place. The balloon soon rose into the sky once again.

"They're selling rides on that thing," Clint observed. "I always wondered what the world looked like from a couple hundred feet up in the air."

"You're not thinking of going up in that thing are you?" Martha inquired.

"Why not?" Clint grinned. "I've got a nickel."

"That Bolo character is probably lurking somewhere in the circus," she stated. "What if he recognizes you?"

"Well," the Gunsmith mused. "Sometimes you handle a bunch of crooks by going after them and sometimes you try to get them to come after you. Figure this time I'll try both techniques. One or the other is bound to get some sort of results."

"Or it could get you killed."

"Worried about me?" He smiled.

"You know I am."

"Well, if I make myself bait as well as a thorn in Feltrinelli's side," Clint began, "it might keep the bastard too busy to pay much heed to you. Are you still determined to go through with this?"

"What do you think?" Martha asked.

"I think you'd better be damn careful," he warned. "If you make one mistake those bastards won't think twice about killing you."

"I'll be careful," she assured him.

"You remember what I told you about these guys?" Clint added, still hoping to discourage her. "Your sister said they raped her . . ."

"I don't think they'll try anything like that while the circus is so close to a town. I don't intend to be with them when they pull out."

"Yeah." The Gunsmith nodded. "Let's hope we can wrap this business up by tomorrow morning."

He glanced up at *The Black Moon*. A chill traveled along his spine. The Gunsmith had never tangled with enemies like this before. How do you fight opponents who can silently sail through the sky like great vultures?

For a moment the globe-shaped balloon seemed to transform into a giant black skull which leered down at Clint Adams, inviting him to his death.

SIXTEEN

The Gunsmith and Martha parted company at the local livery. While Clint paid the hostler to take care of his wagon and horses, the girl slipped out the back of the rig and quietly left the livery. The Gunsmith then headed over to the sheriff's office.

"So you're the Gunsmith, eh?" Sheriff Clu Kingsdale remarked after Clint introduced himself to the lawman. "Heard that you'd taken to traveling around in a wagon, fixing guns and all."

"That's how I make my living, Sheriff," Clint confirmed.

"Well, I doubt that you'll make much of a profit in Brady for the next day or two," Kingsdale told him. "Reckon you noticed there's a circus in town. Kinda rough competition for any business, eh?"

"Yeah," the Gunsmith admitted. "Maybe I'll just hang around for a day or two and go see the show myself as long as I'm in town."

"As long as you don't start any trouble. But I don't give a good hoot in hell what sort of reputation you have as a fast gun, Adams. Don't give me any reason to regret the fact you rode into Brady, eh?"

"Is everybody in town as friendly as you, Sheriff?" Clint asked dryly.

"I run a nice quiet little town, Adams," Kingsdale told him. "I don't like anything ruining that. Can't say as I'm real fond of quick-draw artists who decide they're too good to be lawmen either."

"That's not why I quit wearing a badge, fella." Clint shrugged. "But I don't figure I owe you any explanations. Doubt if you'd listen to me anyway."

The Gunsmith turned to leave the office, eager to put some distance between himself and the obnoxious lawman.

"Adams!" Kingsdale called. "I don't rightly believe you're just a traveling gunsmith. Make pretty good money selling your quick-draw skill, I reckon. But if somebody hired you to come gunning for someone in Brady, you best ride on right now, eh?"

"Sheriff." Clint sighed. "I've heard enough of your big mouth for one day. If I get an urge to listen to an idiot trying to talk tough, I'll pay you another visit before I leave, eh?"

The Gunsmith decided he could use a cold beer to cool off his temper after his brief conversation with Sheriff Kingsdale. He headed for the local saloon, ordered a beer and carried it to a table where he sat with his back to the wall as he sipped the foamy brew.

"Dumb," he muttered, disgusted with himself for losing his temper with Kingsdale.

The Gunsmith was about to go up against a gang of criminals that were probably more cunning and dangerous than anything he'd confronted since his encounter with the Lacombe Syndicate in New Orleans.* His only ally was a young girl and their plan was risky, requiring them to play

*The Gunsmith #23: The Riverboat Gang.

the hand dealt them after the initial contact with the circus was made.

And Clint had butted heads with the local lawman. That had been careless. The Gunsmith knew he couldn't afford to make mistakes when he was pitted against a well-organized group of outlaws who were as clever as Feltrinelli's people appeared to be.

Clint left the saloon after having his single beer and headed for the only hotel in town. He paid for a room and took his saddlebags and Springfield carbine upstairs. Locking his valuables in the room, Clint checked his .45 and New Line hideout gun once more before he left the hotel.

"I am Sergio Feltrinelli," the balloonist declared, executing a curt formal nod. "I welcome you aboard *The Black Moon.*"

The Gunsmith gazed into the face of the master criminal he had come to destroy. Feltrinelli presented a strikingly dignified appearance as he stood in the basket of the aerostat, his back straight, shoulders level and head held proudly high. He was dressed in a black cotton suit and matching derby, his right hand fisted around the handle of an oak cane.

Feltrinelli's face was lean, with sunken cheeks, thin lips and a sleek nose. His black hair was laced with silver at the temples; his eyes seemed to be as black as the balloon he piloted.

Perhaps it was Clint's imagination, but those black eyes seemed to radiate cold intelligence. The Gunsmith had seen such eyes before. They were void of warmth and human compassion. They were the eyes of a man who had lost part of his soul to ambition and greed.

Clint managed to smile at Feltrinelli as he climbed over

the hoop into the basket. He glanced at the roustabouts who held down the aerostat while the passengers boarded. They were hard-faced, surly young men. Clint figured they were all bottom-of-the-barrel gunmen, small-time outlaws who were too dumb and cowardly to do much of anything unless somebody else told them how to do it.

Two other passengers had entered the basket with the Gunsmith. A short fat man with a bald head nervously wiped his brow with a sweat-stained handkerchief. He looked like he was already having second thoughts about the balloon ride.

The other passenger was a young man with unruly blond hair, a wiry physique and a pair of wire-rimmed glasses perched on the bridge of his nose. Unlike the heavy-set man, he seemed to be delighted as he cheerfully addressed the balloonist.

"Don Feltrinelli?" he began. "I'd like to say that it is a pleasure and an honor to meet you, sir."

"Of course," the Don replied simply, waving a hand at his men.

The gesture was a signal to release the balloon. The airship immediately began to ascend. The Gunsmith found the sensation pleasant, like floating weightless in a dream. Yet he was wide awake and he really was drifting up to Heaven.

Probably about as close as I'll ever get, he thought.

He gazed down over the hoop. The people on the ground below seemed to shrink as the balloon rose higher. The town of Brady resembled a collection of doll houses. Even the big top appeared to be a small blob of white canvas from Clint's observation point.

"The craft you are riding in is an aerostat," Feltrinelli began, lecturing in a bored monotone, "which means it is supported by the buoyancy of the air just as a boat is supported by the buoyancy of water. Hot air balloons are also called *montgolfiers*, in honor of the Montgolfier Brothers who flew the first successful balloon on June 5, 1783. Joseph Montgolfier was inspired when he watched smoke rise from the burning remnants of his father's paper mill. If smoke could rise through cooler air, he reasoned perhaps smoke in a sack could raise the container. . . .''

"I bet his old man wished he'd been inspired to put out the fire instead of just standing by and watching his mill burn up,'' the fat man said with a chuckle.

"History doesn't include that information, sir,'' Feltrinelli said with an icy glare. "The first balloon flight was in Annonay, France. It carried no human passengers, although a sheep, a duck and a rooster were on board.''

"La Montgolfière, the first balloon,'' the young man on board added eagerly, "was so uncontrollable it had to be shot down with cannon fire. Still, Jean François Pilâtre de Rozier made the first manned flight in a balloon later that autumn in 1783.''

"Would you care to give the lecture instead, young man?'' Feltrinelli asked in a cold hard voice.

"Uh, no, sir,'' the youth replied sheepishly. "I didn't mean to offend you. It's just that I've studied aeronautics for years and I'm really thrilled to be here and to get to meet you in person, Mr. Feltrinelli.''

"How gratifying. I'm glad to have been an inspiration to you, Mr. . . . ?''

"Dolby,'' the young man answered. "Dexter Dolby. I'm the local veterinarian here in Brady, but I'm really interested in research and science.''

"I see,'' Feltrinelli said dryly. "Since you're a veterinarian, perhaps you'd care to take a look at one of our big cats. It's the only leopard in the Circus Incredible. The cat is very old and seems to have lost its hearing.''

"A deaf leopard?" Dolby frowned. "I'm afraid I wouldn't know what to do about that."

"A pity." Feltrinelli sighed.

"There seems to be a lot of heat coming from that balloon," the fat man remarked. "Is that normal?"

"It is a *hot air* balloon," Feltrinelli replied. "You will please note the burner attached to the ring at the neck of the bag. It burns coal gas which fills the balloon and allows us to rise based on the principles observed by Joseph Montgolfier which I explained before."

"Sure." The chubby man nodded. "That means this thing is safe, right? I mean, it won't blow up or anything? I've heard of that happening in these things."

"Don't worry," Dolby assured him. "That can't happen when coal gas is used to fill the balloon. You see, some balloons use hydrogen instead. Now, that can catch fire, burn and explode. In fact, Pilâtre de Rozier, the first man to fly in a balloon, was also the first to be killed in one when the hydrogen balloon he and Jules Romain piloted caught fire and exploded in June 1785."

"You have studied the subject, haven't you, Mr. Dolby?" Feltrinelli commented with irritation.

"Uh, yes, sir," Dolby said quietly.

"But our third passenger has been strangely silent," Feltrinelli remarked, turning toward Clint. "You don't seem to be as thrilled as Mr. Dolby or as frightened as our obese friend here."

"Now see here," the stocky man complained, "there's no need to be insulting. . . ."

"I'm talking to the other gentleman, sir," Feltrinelli snapped.

"The balloon trip is just fine, fella," Clint told him. "I've got no complaints. I figure I'm getting my nickel's worth."

"I'm so glad." Feltrinelli almost yawned.

"I do have one question," the Gunsmith added. "Do you always treat people like dirt?"

A cruel smile appeared on the man's colorless lips. "If I've given you that impression, I apologize, Mr. . . . ?"

"Adams."

"*Clint Adams?*" the fat man asked fearfully, staring at the scar on Clint's cheek. "The Gunsmith?"

"I'd just as soon you didn't call me that, friend." Clint sighed.

"But don't you enjoy being famous, Mr. Adams?" Feltrinelli asked with amusement.

"Not really," the Gunsmith replied. "How do you like it?"

"The Feltrinelli Family has been renowned as acrobats throughout Europe for more than five centuries. Fame and success have always been part of my legacy."

"If you're an acrobat," the heavy-set passenger began, "how come you're flying this thing?"

"You would have to ask that," Feltrinelli said coldly.

He suddenly raised his walking stick as if to strike out at the man. The fat passenger cried out in alarm and tried to recoil, colliding with the rim of the basket. Feltrinelli viciously lashed out with the cane, hitting his own right leg hard. His expression revealed bitterness and anger, but no pain.

"I suffered an accident ten years ago," he explained. "I fell from a trapeze. It was nearly fatal. Spinal damage occurred. This leg is paralyzed. Naturally, my career as an acrobat was over."

Feltrinelli looked away from the others and gazed down at the circus big top below. "However, I still have the tradition of my family to continue. I supervise the performances of my sons and I can still fly in this contraption.

It isn't the same as a trapeze, of course, but . . ."

He suddenly noticed a figure on the ground beneath the hovering balloon. A woman dressed in a man's shirt and Levi's was performing a series of handsprings before an admiring crowd. She then executed some cartwheels, followed by a back flip, somersaulting in the air before landing in a perfect split.

"Hey," the chubby man declared, "she's pretty good. Not hard to look at either."

"Yes," Feltrinelli remarked. "If you gentlemen have no more questions, we shall return to earth. I hope you've enjoyed your flight and I hope you will come to the circus later this evening. Show begins at seven o'clock. Thank you."

The balloon began to descend. Clint Adams stared down at Martha Harlow who was now walking on her hands to the delight of the applauding crowd. She had succeeded in getting Feltrinelli's attention, but Clint felt even more apprehensive about their plan than he had before. Martha would have to be careful. Her life wouldn't be worth a prairie dog whisker if Feltrinelli suspected a trick.

SEVENTEEN

When the balloon touched ground the fat man climbed out of the basket as rapidly as his bulk would allow. Clint Adams followed, swinging his long legs over the hoop. Dexter Dolby lingered for a moment, probably hoping to speak with Feltrinelli about aeronautics in more detail, but he realized the man wasn't sympathatic to his interest in science. Reluctantly, Dolby left the carriage.

"Feltrinelli isn't apt to win any personality awards," the Gunsmith remarked to Dolby.

"I guess I should have kept my mouth shut," the youth said with a sigh. "I sort of got carried away. God, I love flying in a balloon. Was this your first time, Mr. Adams?"

"Yeah," Clint replied.

"This makes my fourth fixed flight," Dolby declared with a grin. "But I once served as crew with the Bisby balloon in a free flight from Kansas to Idaho."

"You must know a lot about balloons," Clint commented.

"Wish I knew a lot more," Dolby said. "My father knew John Wise. He was a balloonist and an inventor. He made the rip cord safety device for quick, safe descent in a balloon. He once flew his aeronautic machine, the *Atlantic*, from St. Louis to New York and set a world record."

"I remember." Clint nodded. "It was before the War. I was just a kid then myself, but I remember."

"Yeah." Dolby sighed. "But most of the balloonists are still Europeans. Sure wish we had more American aeronauts."

"We will," the Gunsmith assured him. "With fellas with your kind of interest in flying, I'm sure of it."

He glanced over his shoulder. Feltrinelli had gotten out of the balloon and was talking to Martha. Then they walked to the big top together, the circus master leaning heavily on his cane as he dragged his lifeless leg.

The Gunsmith watched the pair enter the tent. Apparently Martha had told Feltrinelli she was looking for a job as a circus acrobat and he had either decided to hire her on the spot or to discuss possible employment.

Clint tried not to dwell on what could go wrong. How much had Jane Harlow told the circus people about her sister? Martha was using a false name of course, but would someone suspect her true identity based on Jane's description? Jane may have even had a picture of her sister. If so, how recently had it been taken? Hell, one of Feltrinelli's employees might have even met Martha in the past.

Then a face appeared at the canvas entrance of the tent. Savage eyes burned with bestial fury in a dark face deformed by twin networks of ornate scars. The Gunsmith was not likely to forget that face.

Bolo had spotted him.

Clint Adams smiled at the aborigine and nodded to confirm mutual recognition. The primitive Bolo seemed about to charge from the tent, ready to attack the Gunsmith in broad daylight. Then he abruptly vanished from view.

Well, Clint thought, *something is bound to happen now*.

"Do you intend to be in town long, Mr. Adams?" Dexter Dolby asked.

"For a day or two," the Gunsmith replied. "And call me Clint."

"Sure." Dolby grinned. "I'm Dex. Buy you a drink, Clint?"

"That's an offer I hardly ever turn down," the Gunsmith said with a nod.

EIGHTEEN

Everyone in Brady and other communities and farms in the county had heard about the circus. Such events were rare in the West. People swarmed to see the exotic entertainment promised by the advertisements. It was an opportunity to witness things most of them had never seen before and a chance to break the monotony that filled the lives of many.

The Gunsmith and Dexter Dolby were among the audience that assembled on rows of benches surrounding the huge sawdust-covered circle inside the big top. A man dressed in a khaki uniform with stovepipe boots and a white helmet strode to the middle of the ring.

"Good evening ladies and gentlemen," he announced with a smile. "Welcome to the Circus Incredible. I am your ringmaster for the evening—Franco the Fearless. Later, you will see that my title is more than just an idle boast.

"Indeed," he continued, "tonight you will see many things that will thrill and amaze you. You'll witness acts of unbelievable skill and extraordinary courage. For this is the Circus Incredible. Tonight you will see the most unusual performers in the world. And to begin our lineup of international talent, I introduce to you . . . The Amazing Yamoto!"

A small Oriental dressed in a black kimono entered the ring. The Japanese formally bowed to the audience while a pair of roustabouts hastily set up a large board, six feet high and four feet wide.

Then Martha Harlow stepped forward.

The Gunsmith was stunned to see the girl as part of Yamoto's act—whatever it was. She was stunning, dressed in pink tights that offered a generous view of cleavage and beautifully displayed her long shapely legs. Several cowboys in the audience whistled in crude appreciation of her beauty as the girl stood before the board, arms extended from the sides.

Yamoto suddenly whirled and swung an arm at the girl. Metal flashed as a knife hurled toward Martha. The Gunsmith tensed in horror for that split second before the blade struck. The knife lodged in the board, less than three inches from Martha's neck.

The Japanese quickly drew more knives from his robe, hurling them rapidly at the target. The Gunsmith held his breath as the blades hissed through air before slamming into wood to form an outline around Martha's lovely body.

Clint recalled reading about a Japanese throwing knife called a *kozuka*. It was the first weapon taught to the samurai knight-warriors of Japan.

Was this Yamoto a samurai? It seemed impossible that such a warrior could wind up in an obscure little circus. Yet, Clint had heard that there was supposed to be at least one samurai roaming the American West. These stories varied. Some claimed the samurai was on a mission of vengeance, bound by the code of Bushido. Others said he was in the company of a beautiful young girl. Both versions claimed the samurai was a noble, brave and fierce warrior.

It seemed unlikely that Yamoto could be such a man.

Clint wondered if the knife-thrower was a *ronin* or merce-
nary samurai who no longer had an allegiance to a war-
lord. Whoever and whatever he was, Yamoto was one hell
of a knife artist. Still, the Gunsmith was relieved when his
act ended. Martha, a bit pale, but without a scratch or nick
from the knives, managed to smile and bow before the
crowd.

The following acts didn't fill the Gunsmith with dread,
although he watched with interest, aware that every performer in the Circus Incredible was a potential opponent.
However, the next act didn't seem very threatening. A
rather poor juggler stood in the center of the ring and tried
to keep four balls from dropping. He failed twice and
earned plently of boos in the process. Clint guessed the
guy was probably one of the hootowls on Feltrinelli's
payroll who used to entertain his friends and family by
juggling oranges. *Get some more practice*, Clint thought.
Better yet, go home.

The next performer was billed as Ace Bacall, the
World's Greatest Sharpshooter. Although the tall lean
man with long yellow hair and a flowing mustache, rem-
iniscent of George Armstrong Custer, was dressed in a
ridiculous buckskin costume that had been bleached
white, no one laughed at Ace Bacall. He had a reputation
as a sharpshooter, sure enough, but Clint was surprised to
see Bacall publicly boasting of his prowess with a rifle.

Ace Bacall had been a bounty hunter of the worst kind.
He had a reputation as a dry-gulcher who never faced a
man in a fair fight. Every time Ace Bacall hauled in a man
for a reward, the body was draped over a saddle with a
bullet hole in his back. Bacall had developed a dubious
skill nonetheless. It was said he could put a bullet through
a man's heart by shooting him under the left shoulder
blade from four hundred yards.

Feltrinelli must not have known about Bacall's reputation or he would have surely told him to change his name. Featuring a notorious dry-gulcher would hardly be a credit to the Circus Incredible. Bacall didn't seem to mind the cold reception he got from the audience. In fact, he seemed to enjoy it as he saluted the crowd with the Winchester rifle that had helped him earn his fame.

Bacall performed a series of sharpshooting stunts which, the Gunsmith grudgingly admitted, revealed genuine skill as a marksman. The ex-bounty hunter turned circus star fired his rifle at a revolving wheel with clay pipes mounted on the rim. Each shot exploded a pipe until all were gone.

"Now, folks"—Bacall turned to the audience—"ya'll see that bail of hay over yonder? Well, there's a match stickin' outta it. I'm gonna light it. Ya'll give me three shots to try to get the match. Fair enough?"

Bacall aimed his Winchester at the bail and squeezed off a shot. The audience applauded when the bullet failed to ignite the match. Everyone hoped the trick wouldn't work. The next shot disappointed the crowd. Flame flared from the match. A roustabout doused the hay with water before the fire could spread.

"Thanks, folks." Ace Bacall laughed. "See ya'll around."

The next act featured Franco the Fearless who proved to be the lion tamer. Still clad in his safari outfit with a holstered revolver on his hip and a whip in his hand, Franco entered a large cage just beyond the center ring.

Franco waved and smiled at the audience. He doffed his helmet and bowed deeply. Clint could see why Franco had been chosen to be the ringmaster. The guy seemed to be the only member of the circus with a pleasant personality . . . or at least the ability to present that appearance.

Now an iron gate rose and the lions began to enter the

main cage. Three males with great shaggy manes and a sleek lioness began to jog around the diameter of the cage, probably stretching their muscles after being cooped up in a smaller compartment awaiting showtime.

Franco snapped orders at the cats as he cracked the whip, taking care not to actually strike the lions. The beasts had been taught to respond to the noise of the lash. To literally whip one of the lions might cause the animal to attack. Franco would be lucky to manage to draw his pistol before the lion could pounce. And Clint doubted that a single bullet would stop such a large, fierce animal unless it hit the cat right between the eyes.

Luckily, the beasts were accustomed to their trainer and the stunts expected of them. The lions sat up, rolled over and lined up on command. The tricks were fairly simple, but Franco's act still got the biggest applause thus far, probably because none of the spectators would have cared to take such a risk—including the Gunsmith.

"Thank you, ladies and gentlemen," Franco declared when he emerged from the cage. "I must say, I deserve your applause."

The remark earned a burst of laughter from the crowd.

"And now," Franco announced, "I present Bolo the Wild Man who will demonstrate the most unbelievable skill with primitive weapons you will ever witness."

The Australian aborigine strode into the center of the ring, carrying a long spear in his fist and the boomerang thrust into his loincloth. He glanced over the audience as if trying to locate a face in the crowd . . . or so it seemed to Clint.

The roustabouts followed Bolo. One held a basket of apples while the other plucked out the contents and began to throw the fruit at the aborigine. Bolo's spear lashed out in a blur, the blade slashing the apples before they could reach him. Sliced fruit fell at Bolo's bare feet.

The man with the basket then threw the container into the air. With a bestial roar, Bolo hurled his lance. It struck the basket, piercing it in midair. The spear sailed into the board formerly used in Yamoto's knife act. The point slammed into wood. The shaft vibrated from the impact, the punctured basket still dangling from it.

The demonstration earned a few gasps and little applause from the audience. The next portion of Bolo's act, however, got a much stronger response from the crowd. He suddenly drew his boomerang and threw it at them. The tent was filled with alarmed voices as the weapon whirled over the heads of the startled spectators.

Clint Adams immediately ducked low, his hand clawing at the grips of his .45 Colt. It didn't seem likely that Bolo could have singled him out of the crowd or that he was accurate enough to aim his boomerang at Clint with so many other heads in the way. Still, it would have been a perfect "accident" if the weapon happened to crack Clint's skull at that moment.

However, the weapon didn't hit anyone. It made a single smooth revolution above the cowering heads of the crowd and hurled back to its owner. Bolo's hand snaked out to snare the boomerang with apparent ease. The audience applauded, stunned by the unique demonstration.

Franco stepped beside the aborigine with a lit candle in hand as he extended his arm. Bolo again hurled his boomerang. The Gunsmith wasn't taking any chances. He ducked again as the device spun above the heads of the audience once more. The boomerang returned to its owner . . . after whirling past the candle closely enough to blow out the flame.

Bolo deftly caught his boomerang once more. He seemed to ignore the appluase of the dumbfounded crowd as he moved to the spear and yanked it free of the board. He marched away, paying no attention to the audience.

"We hope you have enjoyed tonight's entertainment," Franco declared. "Now, if you will please file outside, we will present the final and most exciting performance of all—the Fantastic Flying Feltrinelli Brothers!"

The crowd followed instructions and headed for the exit. The Gunsmith and Dexter Dolby were among them. Clint wondered if every one of the performers he'd seen that night was a criminal. He'd clashed with unusual outlaws before, but never such a bizarre assortment.

Well, he thought, *they're different*.

NINETEEN

A collective gasp rose from the onlookers as they stared up at two hot air balloons which floated in the night sky a hundred feet overhead. A trapeze and a short rope ladder dangled from the basket of *The Black Moon* and another aerostat with a dark blue bag and a yellow basket.

Three young men, all slender yet well-muscled and dressed in white tights, swung from the trapeze bars. The aerialists hurled through the sky from one trapeze to the other, their bodies spinning like tops. The crowd cheered as they watched with awestruck admiration the acrobats' skill and courage.

The Gunsmith, however, had other matters on his mind. He figured everyone present, including the members of the circus, would be giving the trapeze act their full attention. Clint took advantage of this distraction and slipped away from the crowd.

He slid under the canvas wall of the big top and crawled under the benches of the deserted tent. Clint wanted to find out more about the circus and he needed evidence to prove that Feltrinelli's group was involved in illegal and murderous operations. Martha had already infiltrated the circus, but Clint would have to find a different way to penetrate the outfit.

The Gunsmith sprawled on the ground and tried to

make himself as comfortable as possible. There was nothing to do but wait.

The crowd left immediately after the conclusion of the trapeze act, but Clint heard the circus people moving about outside the tent. Occasionally, he saw roustabouts walking around inside the big top. To his relief, no one checked the bleachers or remained long inside the big top. Everyone was probably tired and ready to get some sleep.

When all activity ceased, the Gunsmith waited an extra fifteen minutes before finally crawling out from his hiding place. His eyes had adjusted to the dark and he had no trouble slipping out of the tent the same way he'd gotten in.

Clint moved silently among the shadows surrounding the circus site. A half moon and a skyful of stars illuminated the tent and wagons. He wondered where Martha Harlow was. Why had they used the girl for the knife thrower's act? Probably because it would be too dangerous for her to join the other acrobats on the trapeze. Of course, she didn't have an act yet so they'd given her a task which required plently of raw nerve but no real talent . . . unless one calls standing still while knives are thrown at you talent. It sure as hell took guts.

The Gunsmith noticed a campfire located near a couple of cabinlike passenger wagons. The scent of freshly brewed coffee tempted his nostrils. It also warned him that there were probably sentries on duty. Taking care of them became Clint's first problem.

Instead of trying to locate the guards, he simply hid under a wagon and waited for one of the sentries to head toward him. Ten minutes later, he saw a roustabout approach. The man was armed with a crossbow and a sidearm on his hip.

Why do these people use so many crossbows? Clint wondered. He guessed that they didn't want to attract attention with gunshots so close to town. Was this a standard procedure or had Feltrinelli somehow guessed he might have an uninvited visitor that night?

Either way, Clint would have to play the hand however the cards fell.

The sentry actually strolled by the wagon, unaware that the Gunsmith was hidden there. Clint slid his Colt from leather as he watched the guard's legs walk past. Without warning, he reached out and caught one of the man's ankles and pulled hard. The sentry cried out feebly before he fell on his belly.

Clint slithered from his position and quickly chopped the barrel of his revolver across the base of the guard's skull. The man's unconscious body went limp. The Gunsmith heard footsteps as another sentry was drawn by the sound.

The second guard held his crossbow ready, the weapon cocked with a bolt in position. He glanced about, leery of an ambush. Then he spotted his partner seated on the ground with his back propped against a wagon wheel.

"Pete?" he called softly when he noticed the man was still breathing. "What the hell . . . ?"

He didn't hear the Gunsmith's stealthy approach until it was too late. The sentry started to turn when Clint hit him behind the left ear with his Colt. The second guard collapsed with a sigh.

Clint hastily disarmed the pair and used their own belts to bind their wrists to the spokes of wagon wheels. He gagged them with their own bandanas and discarded their revolvers and one crossbow. Clint kept the other cocked with a bolt ready to fire just in case.

The Gunsmith had an annoying problem. He was looking for some sort of evidence, but he didn't have any idea what it might be or where to start his search. Lights burned in the windows of several of the wagons, warning him that not all of the circus personnel were snug in their beds. He couldn't be certain whether or not they had a guard captain who'd check on the sentries either.

Time was against him. Clint had to act quickly and get out. Then he noticed a small wagon-cabin set apart from the other rigs. A warning sign was nailed to it, its legend written in red and easy to read even in dim light: EXPLOSIVES: KEEP OUT.

"Explosives?" Clint whispered. "What the hell do they need explosives for?"

Suddenly, he heard the rustle of cloth. Clint spun to see a roustabout less than ten feet from him. The man held the stock of a crossbow at his shoulder, the weapon aimed at the Gunsmith.

Instinct and battle-honed reflexes took over as Clint snap-aimed his crossbow at the would-be assassin and squeezed the trigger. He'd never fired a crossbow before. The bolt went high and to the right, the steel point slamming into the enemy's shoulder.

The man's crossbow flew from his grasp as he wailed in agony and fell to the ground, clawing at the shaft of the quarrel buried in his shoulder. Alarmed voices filled the campsite.

"Aw, shit," the Gunsmith hissed as he discarded his crossbow and dashed into the night.

TWENTY

"So much for reconnaissance," Clint Adams muttered as he leaned against a wooden porch roof support in front of the hotel.

The Gunsmith had managed to escape unnoticed by the circus personnel before any of them realized what had happened. There was nothing more he could do that night. Clint realized he had accomplished nothing by his trip to the Feltrinelli stronghold except to alert his enemies to expect trouble. Maybe he'd think of something to try next after a good night's sleep.

The Gunsmith entered the hotel and mounted the stairs. As soon as Clint entered the room and closed the door a hand seized him from behind, palm clamped over his mouth, pulling his head back. Instinctively, Clint raised an arm to protect his exposed throat. His assailant's forearm connected. Clint glimpsed the flash of steel in the killer's fist.

The Gunsmith desperately grabbed the wrist behind the knife and rammed an elbow into his opponent's ribs. The killer grunted. He moved the hand from Clint's mouth to his throat, clawing strong fingers at the Gunsmith's windpipe.

Clint held onto the man's wrist with one hand while he used the other to pry at the fingers locked on his throat. He

113

stomped a boot heel into the assailant's instep. The Gunsmith broke the killer's grip from his throat and butted the back of his head into the man's face.

Turning sharply, Clint grabbed the assailant's wrist and twisted hard, forcing the man to drop his knife. He stared into the face of his opponent. It was Yamoto, the Japanese knife thrower.

With a *kiai* shout, Yamoto chopped the side of his left hand between Clint's shoulder blades. Stunned, the Gunsmith loosened his grip long enough for the Japanese to break free. A heel of the palm stroke hit Clint under the jaw and sent him staggering backward.

The Gunsmith had heard enough about Oriental styles of hand to hand combat to know he didn't want to try to take on Yamoto on his terms. Clint swiftly drew his .45 Colt and aimed it at the assassin.

"Freeze!" he snapped.

Yamoto didn't. He lashed a roundhouse kick, knocking the gun from Clint's grasp. The Japanese slashed another edge of the hand chop to the Gunsmith's chest which propelled him across the room. Then Yamoto reached inside his kimono.

The Gunsmith dove to the floor as Yamoto unleashed a *kozuka* throwing knife. The projectile struck a wall, blade buried deeply in plaster. Yamoto's arm flashed again. Clint rolled to the right as another knife slammed into the floor.

Clint scrambled to the cover of a straight-backed wooden chair. Yamoto hurled a third knife which sailed over the Gunsmith's head. Clint grabbed the chair and raised it as a shield. A thrown knife bit into the seat.

The Gunsmith suddenly charged Yamoto and stabbed the ends of two chair legs into the Oriental's stomach and chest. Yamoto stumbled from the unexpected blow, but quickly threw a sidekick at the Gunsmith. Clint blocked the attacking leg with the chair, striking Yamoto's ankle hard.

The Japanese roared and swung a powerful hand chop which broke one of the chair legs, snapping it like a toothpick. The Gunsmith immediately retaliated by lashing a boot into his opponent's crotch. Yamoto gasped and doubled up in agony.

Clint Adams swung the chair as hard and he could, smashing it into the Oriental killer with every ounce of desperate strength at his command. The chair shattered from the force of impact and the tremendous blow knocked the assassin across the width of the room into the window.

Glass and framework burst apart under Yamoto's weight as the Japanese toppled over the sill and plunged outside. He screamed as he fell two stories before landing on the hitching rail in front of the hotel. The impact was so great, the rail broke in two.

So did Yamoto's backbone.

TWENTY-ONE

"I understand you two have already met," Sheriff Clu Kingsdale commented as Feltrinelli entered the lawman's office.

"Yes," the circus master admitted, locking eyes with the Gunsmith. "Mr. Adams and I chatted earlier when he took a ride on *The Black Moon* today."

"Reckon my deputy told you what happened, Mr. Feltrinelli," Kingsdale began wearily. "Adams here claims a feller from your circus tried to kill him."

"Really, Sheriff." Feltrinelli shook his head. "That seems highly unlikely."

"Unlikely or not," Kingsdale said, "Adams threw that knife thrower of yours outta his hotel window about half an hour ago."

"So your deputy told me. He also said Yamoto is dead."

"That's right," Clint confirmed. "He tried to kill me and there wasn't any other way I could stop him."

"Well, Yamoto was always a rather strange sort," Feltrinelli declared. "Had a rather nasty opium habit, I'm afraid. Perhaps he planned to rob Mr. Adams."

"Why me?" the Gunsmith asked.

"You have a reputation as a gunslinger. I suppose Yamoto assumed that meant you've made quite a bit of money that way."

117

"He was waiting behind my door when I entered the room," the Gunsmith stated. "He tried to kill me. . . ."

"It sounds as if you surprised him while he was searching the place for valuables," Feltrinelli replied.

"Reckon that's the only explanation that makes sense," Kingsdale agreed. "Unless you got some other theory, Adams."

"Nothing you'd care to hear, Sheriff." The Gunsmith shrugged.

"Then I guess that settles it." Kingsdale yawned. "Sorry to disturb you at this hour, Mr. Feltrinelli. Thanks for clearin' things up for us."

"Yeah," Clint muttered. "Thanks."

"You're welcome." Feltrinelli smiled thinly. "I do feel rather badly about this, Mr. Adams."

"You'll get over it," Clint said dryly.

"I'd like to talk to you about a couple matters," the circus master told him. "Would you care to be my guest for lunch tomorrow?"

"How about making it breakfast instead?" the Gunsmith shrugged. "Here in Brady at the hotel restaurant?"

"If that would make you more comfortable, Mr. Adams."

True to his word, the impresario arrived at the diner the following morning to meet with the Gunsmith. Clint Adams was already seated at a table, his back to the wall. Feltrinelli appeared in the doorway and limped across the threshold.

Three muscular young men followed him. They were dressed identically in white ruffled shirts and black trousers. Only one of them carried a gun, a British Tranter revolver in a belly holster. Feltrinelli led the trio to Clint's table.

"Good morning, Mr. Adams."

"That remains to be seen," Clint replied. "Why'd you bring those three?"

"These are my sons," Feltrinelli explained. "Perhaps you saw them perform on the trapeze last night. You did come to the show last night, didn't you?"

"Oh, yeah," the Gunsmith admitted. "In fact, I was probably the last person to leave."

"I expected as much."

"Figured you would," Clint said.

"Permit me to introduce my sons. Vito, Carlo, and Antony."

The brothers looked very much alike, lean, muscular and darkly handsome with smoldering, hard eyes. Vito appeared to be the oldest and sported a bushy black mustache. Carlo's nose had apparently been broken and never recovered. Antony was trying to grow a mustache, but he'd only succeeded in sprouting a few thin whiskers on his lip which created a catfishlike appearance.

"I thought *you* wanted to talk to me," Clint said. "Not your entire family."

"Do they make you uncomfortable, Mr. Adams?" the impresario asked.

"I'd rather they sat at a different table," Clint replied. "And if they don't, I'll leave."

"You don't want to talk to me?" Feltrinelli frowned.

"I don't want your son pulling a gun on me under the table." Clint tilted his head at the Tranter on Carlo's belt.

"Very well." He spoke to his sons in Italian. They nodded and moved to another table.

"That's better," Clint said as Feltrinelli rejoined the Gunsmith.

"Shall we speak bluntly?"

"Might be nice for a change."

"I know you infiltrated my circus last night," Feltrinelli declared. "You struck two of my men over the head and wounded another with a crossbow bolt."

"Why do you think it was me?"

"Because Bolo recognized you. Bolo also told us about your encounter with the girl. You killed three of my men that night."

"And they killed the girl," the Gunsmith stated. "Acting on your orders."

"Why is she important to you, Mr. Adams?"

"I don't think you'd understand."

"Probably not." The Italian shrugged. "But the girl is dead. Nothing you can do can change that."

"I can make sure you don't kill any more innocent people."

"If you're convinced I'm guilty of such crimes why haven't you gone to the authorities?" Feltrinelli asked with a thin smile.

"You know why," Clint replied flatly. "I don't have enough evidence—yet."

"Nor will you get it in the future. You won't catch us off guard again, I promise you that. And I trust you realize that even the Gunsmith could not storm my circus single-handed and defeat all my men."

"If you're so sure I can't cause you any trouble," Clint began, "why did you send Yamoto to kill me?"

"An overreaction," Feltrinelli admitted. "And a mistake. I can't send another man to kill you because it would appear too suspicious now. So you can see, we're both stalemated."

"Perhaps." The Gunsmith shrugged. "What do you expect to accomplish by this meeting?"

"You've cost me four men. Although you'd certainly lose in the end, I don't want any more trouble from you. The Circus Incredible is moving on to another locale today. If you follow and try to cause any more problems, I'll be forced to kill you.''

''You've made your threat, Feltrinelli,'' Clint told him. ''Now get the hell away from my table and let me finish my breakfast in peace.''

''Certainly,'' the impresario agreed. ''Just make certain you understand my warning. If you value your life, you'll heed it.''

TWENTY-TWO

If Feltrinelli had known more about the Gunsmith, he would have realized that the attempt to frighten off Clint Adams would only make him more determined to settle his score. When the Circus Incredible folded up its big top and moved on from Brady, the Gunsmith and his wagon was ready to follow.

Of course, Clint couldn't allow the circus to get out of his sight. Martha Harlow was still among the personnel. He had to be close to the circus when she managed to escape from it . . . or if she needed his help to get away.

The circus didn't travel far. The following day, it made camp outside of yet another small town called Logo. Clint rode his wagon into town and took his rig and horses to the local livery stable. After paying the hostler a generous fee to give his property the best of care, the Gunsmith headed for the sheriff's office.

"I thought I'd find you here, Clint," a familiar voice declared.

He turned to see Dexter Dolby approach.

"I didn't expect to see *you*," Clint replied.

"We have something in common," the veterinarian stated, "We're both highly curious by nature . . . and intrigued by a mystery,"

"What mystery are you talking about?" the Gunsmith asked.

"Why don't we talk about this over a drink?"

"If you're buying." Clint shrugged.

The pair entered the only saloon in town. It was a typical small tavern with a simple bar, a few tables and chairs and dirty sawdust covering the floor. Clint and Dolby strode to the bar and ordered two beers.

"Tell me, Clint," Dolby began as they sat at a table, "why are you following the circus?"

"I didn't say I was," the Gunsmith replied.

"You don't have to," the young man said. "The Japanese knife-thrower tried to kill you back in Brady. Then you and Feltrinelli had a meeting the next morning and the circus pulls out. So do you. Doesn't take much deductive reasoning to link everything together."

"Have you come up with a theory about why I'd want to follow them?"

"You're hardly the type to want to become a circus performer," Dolby mused. "That means you and Feltrinelli must have some sort of war going on."

"Why are you interested?" Clint asked suspiciously.

"You think I might be working for him?" Dolby chuckled.

"Yamoto didn't have any trouble finding out where I was staying."

"You didn't tell me," Dolby stated. "They probably assumed you were at the hotel and checked the register when they broke in."

"Okay," the Gunsmith began. "If you're not an agent for Feltrinelli, why are you getting involved in this business?"

"I told you before that I'm interested in seeing American advancements in aeronautics," Dolby explained. "If Feltrinelli is a criminal, he has to be stopped—especially if he's using his balloons for evil purposes."

"You figure that's what he's up to?"

"I think it's possible," Dolby replied. "Hot air balloons have already been used for warfare. Napoleon used them in 1794. There was even talk of a possible invasion of England by a fleet of balloons. That notion was too crazy even for Napoleon to agree to."

"Why?" Clint asked.

"Because the balloons would have been shot down by cannon fire."

"But you think a balloon could be used to commit a crime?"

"Of course," Dolby answered. "And crimes involving a hot air balloon would reflect on aeronauts throughout the country. You know how the newspapers twist facts around. Imagine what they'd do with such a story."

"I'm the fella they labeled the Gunsmith," Clint reminded him. "I know what you're talking about."

"Well, I don't know what we're up against," Dolby admitted. "Maybe you can explain it to me."

"You *don't* know is right," the Gunsmith told him. "A lot of people have already been killed since this business began. Are you sure you want to get involved?"

"I'm here, aren't I?"

Clint Adams told Dolby about the bank robbery in Wido and the multiple murders there. He explained how he'd encountered Jane Harlow and witnessed her death, but he decided not to tell Dolby about Martha, just in case.

Of course, Clint didn't believe Dolby was an enemy or he wouldn't have told him anything. He was prepared to trust Dolby to a degree, but not if it would put Martha in more potential danger than she was already in.

"Jesus," Dolby whispered. "What are we going to do?"

"I'm still thinking about it," the Gunsmith confessed.

"Adams!" a harsh voice barked.

Both men looked up at a stocky man with a broad face who pushed through the batwings to confront the pair. His hand dangled beside the butt of a Smith & Wesson revolver on his hip. The stranger glared at the Gunsmith as he stepped closer.

"My name's Walter Benson," he announced. "That name mean anything to you, Adams?"

"Should it?" Clint asked.

"Maybe you don't remember," Benson said. "You killed my cousin five years ago."

"Your cousin?" the Gunsmith raised his eyebrows. "Uh-huh, Feltrinelli sent you, didn't he?"

"Nobody had to send me, Adams," Benson snarled. "I'm going out into the street. You'd better be ready to face me like the big man you're supposed to be, 'cause if you don't draw, I'll blast a hole through you anyway."

Benson turned and marched to the batwings.

"Hey, fella," the Gunsmith called to him.

The man turned and stared hatefully at Clint in silent acknowledgment.

"Is Feltrinelli going to pay for your funeral?" Clint asked.

Benson spat in contempt and stomped outside.

Dexter Dolby turned to the Gunsmith.

"Are you going to face him, Clint?" he asked.

"I don't think there's any other choice," the Gunsmith replied as he rose from his chair. "If I don't take him on now, he'll find me later . . . or Feltrinelli will try something else."

"Are you sure the Don sent him?"

"It'd be a hell of a coincidence if he didn't," Clint commented. "What I'm wondering is whether this Benson character really thinks he can take me or if there's something else involved."

"Such as?"

"Guess I'll find out."

He crossed the barroom and pushed through the bat-wings. The citizens of Logo were hastily rushing for cover, clearing the street for the lethal contest which was about to take place. Walter Benson stood in the middle of the street, waiting for the Gunsmith.

Clint Adams stepped off the plankwalk and approached his adversary.

TWENTY-THREE

The Gunsmith had made the long walk many times before. Literally dozens of men had challenged him in the past. The "legend of the Gunsmith" as it appeared in the newspapers, actually chronicled less than half of the gunfights he had survived. Ironically, most historians would consider the printed reports to be exaggerations. In truth, Clint Adams probably fought more duels than any man who ever lived.

But the Gunsmith's success as a pistolman was not due only to his uncanny speed and accuracy with a gun. He watched his opponent for any telltale signal that the man was about to make his move. Clint observed everything, especially the eyes of his adversary and a sudden shift of the man's shoulders which telegraphed a rapid movement of the arm and hand.

As Clint walked into the street to confront Walter Benson, he slowly scanned the surrounding buildings. He glimpsed the faces of a dozen spectators watching from windows and doorways. Their expressions revealed apprehension, fear, excitement and, most of all, fascination.

Then Clint saw the dull gleam of sunlight on gunmetal behind the sign that bore the legend HOTEL.

A blond-haired head rose up from the sign. The face of

Ace Bacall stared down at Clint as the dry-gulcher aimed his Winchester at the Gunsmith.

Clint whirled, his Colt appearing in his hand so suddenly it seemed to have materialized in his fist by magic. He fired two rapid double-action rounds into the hotel sign. Bacall screamed and tumbled from his shelter to fall to the ground four stories below.

Walter Benson had desperately drawn his S&W and hastily pointed it at Clint. The Gunsmith pivoted, his body in a low crouch as he swung his pistol toward the gunman. Benson was still thumbing back the hammer of his revolver when Clint's Colt roared twice more. The impact of two .45 caliber slugs in the chest sent Benson hurtling backward. He crashed to the ground, the S&W in his fist still unfired.

"Jesus God!" a portly, middle-aged man with a tin star on his shirt cried as he waddled into the street. "What the hell is goin' on?"

"It's over now," Clint replied, holstering his six-gun.

"Holy Hannah," the sheriff gasped, gazing at the two corpses in the street. "Did you kill these fellers?"

"I put bullets in them both and I don't think they're just holding their breath, Sheriff."

"Don't get sassy with me, feller," the lawman huffed. "I've a mind to arrest you for murder—"

"Self-defense," Clint stated. "Plenty of witnesses to back that up. Reckon the whole town saw it happen except you."

"Nobody told me there was gonna be a gunfight," the sheriff complained.

"It was sort of a spur of the moment affair," the Gunsmith explained. "Maybe you should send a message to the guy who runs the circus that set up outside of town today."

"What?" The baffled lawman frowned. "What should I contact him for?"

"They'd better know that another one of their performers won't be able to participate in tonight's show."

"Their names were Benson and Bacall," Sheriff Samuels told Feltrinelli. "The Gunsmith sent 'em both to the big sleep. The sort you never wake up from."

Feltrinelli gazed down at the lifeless bodies stretched out on the undertaker's twin tables. He sighed wearily and turned to face Clint Adams.

"You must be a remarkable marksman. Would you be interested in a job with my circus?"

"I'd sooner join a pack of rabid wolves for dinner," the Gunsmith replied dryly.

"Uh," the lawman began awkwardly, "Mr. Felt-anelly?"

"*Feltrinelli*," the impresario corrected.

"Yessir." Samuels nodded. "Clint Adams claims these two fellers both worked for you. Is that right?"

"It's half accurate," Feltrinelli answered. "True, Ace Bacall was featured as a sharpshooter, but I've never seen this other man before."

"Funny how they managed to get together and decide to try to kill me, isn't it?" Clint remarked.

"Hold on a minute, Adams," Samuels began. "Everybody knows that Ace Bacall was a stinkin' regulator who specialized in shootin' fellers in the back."

"You figure he was going to shoot me just to keep in practice?" Clint asked. "Check your wanted posters, Sheriff. There's no price on my head . . . unless someone has done so privately."

The Gunsmith glared at Feltrinelli.

"Really, Mister Adams." The Italian shook his head.

"You're not going to make any more groundless accusations, are you?"

"I get the feelin' you fellers know something I don't," the sheriff commented.

"Oh." Feltrinelli sighed. "One of my men tried to rob Adams back in Brady—"

"He tried to kill me," Clint corrected.

"So *you* claim," Feltrinelli said. "In fact, you killed Yamoto—who happened to be the only friend Ace Bacall had among the circus personnel."

"Oh, shit," the Gunsmith muttered. "Now you're going to try to convince us that Bacall planned to avenge Yamoto's death and got Benson to help him try to set me up to be shot in the back."

"Well," Samuels began, "Bacall had a reputation as a dry-gulcher. Sounds like somethin' he might do, if you ask me."

"Sure it makes sense." Clint laughed, surprising Feltrinelli and Samuels. "Not much sense, but enough to use for an excuse. It's a nice, simple explanation, right? I didn't know wishful thinking was part of your job, Sheriff."

"Uh . . . look here, Adams . . ." Samuels replied awkwardly.

"Don't get excited," the Gunsmith told him. "I'll go along with your explanation for now."

"Sheriff Samuels," Feltrinelli addressed the lawman, "I'm sure you can see this man is rather hostile toward me. I'm afraid he might be losing his mind. That happens sometimes with gunfighters, doesn't it? All the pressure and jumping at shadows affects them after a few years, correct?"

"I—I wouldn't know," the lawman answered.

"Well, I don't want this man setting foot on my property. If Clint Adams shows his face at my circus, I'll expel him. Since he is obviously a dangerous man, I will order my men to tell him to leave and if he refuses—they'll be instructed to regard it as a direct threat to the lives of my personnel and they will shoot to kill.''

"Well . . . I reckon you'd be acting within your legal rights, Mr. Felty-nelly.''

The Italian opened his mouth to speak, probably to correct Samuels about the pronunciation of his name, but he decided not to bother. Feltrinelli headed for the door.

"Best watch your behavior, Mr. Adams,'' he commented, glancing over his shoulder at the Gunsmith.

"Good advice,'' Clint replied. "Remember it for yourself, fella.''

TWENTY-FOUR

"Feltrinelli told the sheriff he'd have you killed if you set foot on his circus grounds?" Dexter Dolby asked. "And the lawman agreed?"

"What else could he do, Dex?" Clint Adams shrugged.

The young veterinarian had met Clint in the Gunsmith's hotel room to discuss their situation. Clint showed Dolby one of the crossbows he'd confiscated from the enemy to give him an idea of how clever and resourceful their opponent was. He'd also noticed that Dolby didn't carry a gun so he loaned him a Virginia Dragoon pistol from the weapon supply in his wagon.

"The question is: What are we going to do?" Dolby remarked.

"I don't care if his men have been ordered to shoot me down on sight," Clint declared. "I still have to get into that circus again."

"Maybe I should try instead," Dolby suggested.

"Feltrinelli would be too suspicious." The Gunsmith shook his head. "He'd know there had to be a connection between your presence in Logo and my mission against the circus. It would seem to be too big a coincidence to be mere happenstance."

"Well, there's no reason to charge in there tonight," Dolby said. "We've got time to come up with a plan of action."

"There is a reason why I'm in a hurry," Clint said, still unwilling to tell Dolby about Martha Harlow.

"What is it, Clint?"

"I think Feltrinelli is planning something big," the Gunsmith said as an explanation. "Why else would he have such a large amount of explosives stored in one of the wagons."

"I doubt if he's planning a major operation in a tiny town like Logo." Dolby shrugged.

"You're probably right." Clint nodded. "Let's talk this over in the morning and figure out what to do then."

Dolby retired to his room for the evening. The Gunsmith unbuckled his gunbelt and hung it on the head post of the bed and stretched out on the mattress. He stared up at the ceiling, unable to sleep, his thoughts disturbed by concern for Martha. Had the brutes violated her lovely young body? Had they in fact discovered why she was there and already snuffed out her life? Were they attempting to torture information out of her at that very moment?

A knock on the door roused Clint from his grim thoughts. He rose from the bed, instinctively drawing the Colt from its holster, and moved to the door.

"Who is it?" he asked.

"Harvey Miller," a gruff voice declared through the door. "I'm the desk clerk what signed you in, Mr. Adams."

Leery of a trap, Clint held his pistol ready and stood to the side of the door, his back pressed against the wall as he turned the knob with his left hand and eased the door open.

The round face of the desk clerk stared up at him with tiny piglike eyes.

"What do you want, Mr. Miller?" Clint asked.

"There's a lady askin' to see you," the clerk replied. "Don't look like she's your mommy either."

The Gunsmith immediately thought of Martha and yanked open the door. Miller's eyes expanded with fear when he saw the revolver in Clint's fist.

"Where is she?" the Gunsmith asked.

"I'm here, Clint," a woman's voice whispered.

Martha Harlow stood at the head of the stairs, a cattleman's slicker covering her from shoulder to toe. The girl smiled broadly. She didn't appear to be hurt or distraught; Clint sighed with relief.

"I told you to wait downstairs until I called you," Miller snapped at the girl.

"Mister," Martha said flatly, "I don't feel like listening to a bunch of shit from you. Get off my back before I decide to kick you in the balls."

"Women ain't allowed up in these rooms with a feller unless they're married," Miller declared.

"Does that mean women are only allowed to fool around with married men?" the girl asked snidely.

"I've a mind to go tell the sheriff and have him throw you both out of here," Miller warned.

"Clint," Martha began wearily, "why don't you offer this guy five dollars to look the other way."

"Make it ten," Miller insisted.

The Gunsmith paid him. Miller descended the stairs, muttering sourly about the decay of morality as he counted his money. Martha entered Clint's room and closed the door behind her.

"I've been worried sick about you," Clint said as he

took her in his arms. "You okay?"

"I am now," she replied, snuggling against his chest. "I had to get out of there. I just prayed you'd be here at the hotel. Heard that you killed Bacall and one of the roustabouts today, so I knew you were in town."

"You're safe now." Clint kissed her forehead.

"I wasn't really mistreated," Martha told him. "Except I was scared to death when they used me in that knife throwing act. You killed Yamoto too, didn't you?"

"Yeah." Clint nodded. "Are you okay?"

"With Yamoto dead," she began, "they couldn't feature the knife act anymore, so they were starting to rehearse a new acrobat act that would feature me. Not the trapeze. Too risky. Then tonight, one of the Feltrinelli Brothers, the youngest one, hauled me into his cabin and tried to force himself on me."

"Jesus," the Gunsmith whispered.

"I had a hatpin in my hair. I pulled it out and stabbed the kid in the hollow of the throat. He's dead, Clint."

"You had to protect yourself," the Gunsmith told her.

"Found this coat in his closet," Martha explained. "And a hat. I managed to slip past one of the guards while he was pissing on a tree. Couldn't stay there after I killed the Feltrinelli boy."

"Why don't you sit down and rest awhile?" Clint advised.

"No, I'm okay," she assured him. "Just a little shook up. I never killed anyone before."

"I'm just glad you weren't hurt."

"Feltrinelli's people are planning something, Clint," Martha said. "I'm not sure what it is because no one trusted me enough to talk directly to me about whatever they're up to. I think it involves some explosives Feltrinelli has. He told me the stuff was just fireworks for the show, but I overheard somebody else mention dynamite and how they were all going to be rich as kings by the end of the month.''

''Maybe they're planning a string of bank robberies with the balloons,'' Clint mused. ''But the dynamite would alert the local law and pretty soon word of their methods would spread. Folks would be on the lookout for balloons approaching at night. Those baskets aren't bulletproof. They could be shot down before they could reach a bank if people knew what to look for.''

''Maybe Feltrinelli hasn't considered that,'' Martha suggested.

''I doubt that,'' the Gunsmith declared. ''I just thought of it so I'm sure it's occurred to him as well. No, they must have something else in mind. Probably one single job that'll rake in lots of money at once.''

''Clint,'' Martha began, clinging to his arm. ''Don't we have enough evidence against Feltrinelli now?''

''I think so,'' the Gunsmith answered. ''What you've heard, combined with what happened at Wido and my testimony should be enough to get a federal investigation of the circus. I just wish we knew what they had in mind.''

''Right now,'' Martha smiled as she slipped off the cattleman's slicker, ''I'm just glad to be back in your arms.''

Clint allowed his gaze to slowly scan over Martha's magnificent body clad in the skimpy pink circus costume. She grinned happily, pleased by the desire revealed in Clint's eyes.

''I think I'll get comfortable,'' she announced as she sat on the edge of the bed. ''Want to help me take off these slippers?''

Martha slowly crossed one leg over the other, purposefully making her actions as seductive and tempting as possible. The Gunsmith's manhood was erect and straining against the crotch of his trousers as he sat beside her.

Clint pulled off her slipper and let it drop to the floor. His hand caressed the long expanse of silk-clad leg, running his fingers higher from ankle to thigh. His other arm drew her closer and their mouths crushed together.

The Gunsmith's hands stroked Martha's thighs and crotch while his lips moved to her neck. His tongue played along the sensitive flesh behind her ears and along the jawline. Martha hummed with pleasure as she groped at his stiff member and rubbed it gently.

They stripped quickly as the passion both felt increased rapidly. Naked, they sprawled across the mattress. Clint kissed her bare breasts, sucking the hard nipples and gently teasing them with his teeth. Martha found his rigid penis and eagerly assisted it into her hot damp womanhood.

Clint sighed with contentment as he felt himself slide inside her. He gradually rotated his hips while he continued to kiss her neck and breasts. The Gunsmith braced himself on one elbow while his free hand reached down the back of her thigh.

Martha began to gasp and tremble in delight. Clint rammed himself faster and deeper, his hand gripping her buttocks firmly to steady her as he plunged again and again. Martha almost cried out in passion, her teeth clamping on his left shoulder to muffle the sound.

Their bodies convulsed in a joyous orgasm that nearly tore the sheets off the bed. Clint lay across her, pleasantly exhausted, totally spent.

"Oh, my God," Martha whispered. "You're the best lover in the whole wide world."

"Thanks." Clint grinned. "I think you're wonderful too. A real knockout . . ."

The Gunsmith didn't even hear a whisper of the hard object that crashed into the back of his skull. He plunged into unconsciousness so fast, he hardly felt any pain. . . .

Just a fleeting moment of utter terror.

TWENTY-FIVE

A throbbing pain in the back of Clint's skull told him he was still alive. Darkness seemed to swim before his closed eyes, black raven wings flapping in an ebony sky. A sharp pain at the side of his face rocked his head to the side. Another hard slap followed.

"Shit," he spat.

"I see you're regaining consciousness, Mr. Adams," the voice of Feltrinelli spoke from the dark fog. "I'm so glad Bolo didn't hit you too hard."

The Gunsmith's vision cleared. He found himself still naked, but seated in a straight-backed chair in a cramped cabin with Vito Feltrinelli hovering over him. The acrobat's hand flashed, swatting Clint across the face once more.

"That's enough, Vito," the Don instructed. "At least for now."

The young acrobat stepped aside. Clint shook his head to clear it. Don Feltrinelli, Bolo and Carlo were also crowded into the cabin. The youngest Feltrinelli aimed a crossbow at the Gunsmith, a hateful expression twisting his face into an ugly mask.

"Where's the girl?" Clint asked, rubbing the back of his skull. "What have you done with her?"

"She's outside," Feltrinelli replied. "Franco is watching her. I couldn't have her in here with Carlo present. He has a short temper. We're all very upset because she killed my youngest son, but Carlo is too eager to avenge Antony. He'll kill her with his bare hands if he gets the chance."

"None of this is her fault," the Gunsmith said. "I'm responsible."

"She killed my son," the impresario declared. "But I have no doubt that you were responsible for sending her to us. I just wish I had suspected the girl earlier. Poor Antony might still be alive if I had."

"He tried to rape Martha and she acted in self-defense," Clint told him.

"Martha?" Feltrinelli frowned. "She told me her name was Mary Gentry."

"Her real name is Martha Harlow."

"Jane Harlow's sister?" the Don raised an eyebrow. "I should have guessed that two beautiful young acrobatic girls in Idaho might be related. But they didn't seem to resemble each other much."

"How'd Bolo sneak up on me and club me while I was in my room?" Clint asked, wondering if Dexter Dolby had assisted the circus men.

"My friend Bolo is a most remarkable tracker," Feltrinelli explained. "He followed the girl's trail, even her scent, to the hotel. Why would she flee there instead of to the sheriff? The answer was obviously because *you* were staying at the hotel."

"How'd you know the room number?"

"A Mr. Miller willingly supplied the information for a payment of ten dollars." Feltrinelli smiled.

"That's his going rate," Clint muttered. "How'd your pet goon get into the room? I didn't hear the door open."

"Bolo and Vito entered through the window. Child's play for an aborigine and an acrobat. Bolo simply rapped you on the skull with his boomerang and they bundled you up in a blanket and brought you here."

"To the Circus Incredible," Clint muttered.

"Where you've been warned not to trespass," the impresario added. "You'd better put your clothes on, Mr. Adams. It's a bit chilly outside."

He tossed Clint's shirt and pants to him. The Gunsmith hastily pulled on his clothes. "You must be keeping me alive for a reason, Feltrinelli. What is it?"

"I want you to answer a few questions. But first, turn around and put your hands behind your back."

Clint obeyed. Vito quickly slid a rope around the Gunsmith's wrists and prepared to bind them together. Clint tensed his muscles as hard as he could while the acrobat tied his wrists.

"Okay," Clint said as he turned to face his captors. "What do you want to know?"

"Let's join your murderous lady friend outside," Feltrinelli suggested—as if Clint were in a position to refuse the offer.

All five men filed out the door of the wagon cabin. Outside, Franco and Martha were waiting. The girl was once again clad in her tights and slippers. She also had her hands tied behind her back. A dark bruise decorated the left corner of her jaw.

"You bastards," Clint snarled at his captors. "You're real brave at slapping around a woman and attacking a man from behind, but you don't seem to have much of a stomach for a face-to-face fight, do you?"

"We're facing each other now," Vito sneered as he approached the Gunsmith.

The acrobat swung a fist at Clint's face. The Gunsmith weaved his head out of the way. Vito's fist whistled past Clint's ear as he stepped forward and pumped a knee between his opponent's splayed legs. Vito uttered a wheezing gasp, then fell to the ground, clutching his battered genitals. Bolo and Carlo prepared to launch themselves at Clint.

"Stop this nonsense!" the elder Feltrinelli snapped. "We didn't spend the last twenty minutes reviving Adams just to beat him senseless again!"

Carlo helped his brother to his feet. Clint moved to Martha. Except for the bruised jaw, she seemed unharmed. The Gunsmith had recovered from the blow to his skull, but he still didn't have any idea how they could escape.

"All right, Adams," Feltrinelli began. "I want to know exactly what you've discovered about my operation. I want to know who you've talked to and how much you've told them. Finally, I want to know if you have another spy planted in my circus. I doubt that very much, but I want to be certain."

"Let the girl go and I'll talk," Clint said, although he knew it was pointless to try to bargain.

"She murdered my son," Feltrinelli replied. "The most I can do for you is promise you both a quick death instead of a slow, painful one."

"You'll have to come up with a better deal than that." The Gunsmith smiled.

"You amaze me, Mr. Adams." Feltrinelli sighed. "Such arrogance in the face of death. We'll simply have to force you to be agreeable."

''You go to hell, fella,'' Clint said stiffly.

''That's where you'll think you've been by the time this is over,'' the impresario said savagely.

TWENTY-SIX

"Do you know what's wrong with torture, Mr. Adams?" Feltrinelli inquired as he watched Vito lean over the side of the black basket to cut the cords to a sandbag.

"It's painful," the Gunsmith replied as he glanced over the rim of the carriage at the ground more than two hundred feet below.

The Italian, his two sons and Bolo had escorted the Gunsmith and Martha Harlow to *The Black Moon*. After the burners filled the bag with ample coal gas and some sandbag ballast was removed, the balloon rose into the night sky with its passengers—although Clint still didn't know why Feltrinelli had decided to take them for a midnight flight.

"Torture inflicts great bodily damage which can easily put a man in shock," the circus master explained. "Thus it is an unreliable way to extract information . . . at least, if one employs such crude methods as whips and thumbscrews."

Vito wrapped a thick rope around Clint's waist. The Gunsmith managed to raise his arms to avoid having them bound to his sides as the acrobat tied the rope firmly around his midsection.

"Ah," Feltrinelli remarked as he watched the dark blue balloon rise into the sky as well. "I see the other aerostat is now airborne."

"What are you going to do with it?" Martha asked.

"It's flying to the other side of town to set off some Roman candles and plenty of noisy firecrackers," he answered. "That way the entire community of Logo will be watching the fireworks and there will be too much noise for anyone to notice your screams."

The Don gazed down at the circus tent below. "Oh, I could have released the tether line and we could have flown away from here to conduct our business elsewhere, but there would still be a chance of someone hearing it. Hunters or cowboys or whatever. Besides, if Mr. Adams wants to end all of this with a bullet, I want his body found here at the site where he was shot for trespassing."

"Your men should have checked my wagon," Clint declared, stalling for extra time as he tried to work his hands past the ropes which bound his wrists together. Clint had tensed his muscles on purpose when Vito tied them because the bonds were thus somewhat loose when he relaxed the muscles. Even with his hands free, the odds were still in Feltrinelli's favor, but it was the only chance Clint had.

"Why do you say that?" Feltrinelli asked. "What do you have in your wagon that would be of interest to us?"

"A telegraph key and wires that can be hooked up to any telegraph line leading to the capitol," the Gunsmith lied. "And if I don't send off a message to the federal marshals stationed there, they'll know something happened to me."

"Oh, really?" Feltrinelli asked with amusement.

"They're expecting the next message at one o'clock," Clint told him, straining to free his hands. He wasn't certain he could take Bolo without a gun, let alone the two Feltrinelli brothers as well, but at least he'd go down swinging.

"So you're working for the government?"

"If I don't contact them in the next half hour you'll have a small army of feds on your neck before you can get to the next county," Clint warned.

"Mr. Adams"—Feltrinelli sighed—"have you ever wondered what it's like to fall two hundred feet to your death?"

He then nodded at Bolo and Vito. The pair quickly seized Clint and dragged him to the wall of the basket. Martha screamed. Carlo slapped her in the face hard. The Gunsmith struggled hopelessly against the two powerful men who easily hauled him over the side of the basket.

"Son of a bitch!" Clint snarled as he managed to lash a bare foot into Vito's grinning face.

The acrobat fell away from Clint and staggered backward into his father. Bolo, however, was more than strong enough to handle Clint alone. He rolled the Gunsmith over the rim of the basket and shoved hard.

Clint Adams plunged into the night sky.

He felt a torrent of air rip at his clothes and face as he fell. The ground seemed to rocket up toward him. A wild howling wind battered his ears. Then his body seemed to explode from violent impact.

The Gunsmith's torso felt as if it had been cut in two. He panted heavily, arms dangling at his sides. Two things occurred to his panic-fogged mind. The rope tied to his waist had kept him from hitting the ground and he'd finally managed to free his arms—for whatever good that would do now.

"Now you have a preview of the type of death that awaits you, Mr. Adams," Feltrinelli called down to him.

Clint's head seemed to spin as he gasped air into his lungs. The volley of exploding firecrackers in the distance told him that the fireworks display had begun. He stared up the length of the rope which suspended him from the balloon.

"Of course a drop from this height may not be fatal," Feltrinelli continued as his men hauled up the line, raising Clint higher. "You may well survive, Adams. Of course, your body will be broken. Imagine lying helpless, half the bones in your body already shattered, as my sons stomp what life remains from your worthless carcass."

"If you're planning to feature this as part of the ride for your customers," Clint replied, "you'd better modify your speech. Doesn't sound chatty enough. . . ."

They'd almost raised Clint all the way back to the basket when they released the rope. Clint again plunged downward. The drop was farther this time, almost sixty feet, before it ended abruptly. The cord around his waist constricted like a steel band. He was unable to stifle a groan of agony.

Then they hauled him up again.

"Each time will be worse, Adams," Feltrinelli warned. "Perhaps the next time you'll hit the ground."

"Before I've answered your questions?" the Gunsmith croaked.

"I can still ask the girl."

"She doesn't know anything."

"Then perhaps we'll haul you back into the basket and have her take your place on the rope."

"God damn you, Feltrinelli," the Gunsmith hissed.

"How much do you know, Adams?" he demanded. "Tell me about the Army convoy."

The Gunsmith thought quickly, putting evidence together and coming to a likely conclusion. "You intend to attack it in your balloons by dropping dynamite on it.''

"Brilliant, don't you think?'' the Italian said. "They wouldn't expect to be attacked by a pair of circus balloons. Since they're not armed with cannons they won't be able to shoot us down quickly enough to stop us. Rifle fire will just cause a few mild leaks in the balloons. They'll be blown to bits in less than a minute. Now, *why* are we going to attack the convoy?''

Clint recalled that Martha had said one of the circus people had mentioned a fortune that would make them all wealthy. Since the Army was transporting it, that meant it probably wouldn't be silver or cash.

"They're escorting a shipment of gold,'' he said.

"And where are they taking it?''

Clint couldn't come up with any sort of guess.

"You were doing quite well until now, Adams,'' Feltrinelli remarked. "Congratulations on two correct guesses. You see, among my employees are two Army deserters who decided to retire from the service rather than face a firing squad for murdering their sergeant. These men had been stationed at Fort Simms which has been covertly used as a storage center for U.S. government gold. The amount is worth approximately three million dollars.

"On the twenty-second of this month, the gold will be transferred to Fort Knox in Kentucky which will serve as the deposit box for the U.S. treasury. Fort Knox will be impenetrable, but the convoy is vulnerable to the type of attack we intend to launch. Three million in gold. Can you imagine that, Adams?''

"If you're going to get your hands on a fortune that size,'' the Gunsmith began, "why'd you rob the Wido Bank?''

"You know about that, eh?'' Feltrinelli smiled. "Two

reasons, Adams. First, a number of my men thought the balloons were impractical for use in a criminal operation. We had to prove it somehow and robbing the bank solved a problem common to many armies. You can't pay your troops with promises, Adams. Most of the men were impatient to have money in their pockets. When you have greedy, immoral men on your payroll, you make certain they get paid or they might just turn against you.''

"You have a lot of room to accuse anyone of being greedy or immoral, Feltrinelli,'' Clint sneered. "What about your proud family tradition? Or was that more of your bullshit too?''

"After my accident I was unable to perform as an acrobat. My sons and I couldn't get work with the larger circuses in Europe because they didn't think my sons were experienced enough to handle the act without me. I tried to set up my own circus, but no one would finance me. That's how much our tradition meant to the very people who should have cared the most.''

"So you put together a different type of circus,'' Clint said. "One comprised of criminals.''

"Perhaps I'll be able to start a real circus after we acquire our new finances from the cavalry convoy,'' Feltrinelli mused. "But that's not your concern is it, Adams? The future shouldn't concern you—because you have no future. Good-bye, Mr. Adams.''

TWENTY-SEVEN

The Gunsmith realized they were about to drop him—
and this time they'd simply release the rope and let him
smash to the ground in a bone-shattering fall. He had one
chance for survival and only a split second to try for it.

Clint seized the rope in both hands and swung himself
toward the tether line. The rope suspending him went
slack as his tormentors released it. The Gunsmith's
momentum still hurled him to the tether line, his hands
desperately reaching for it.

His fists closed around the rope. Clint snared the cable
between his feet and hung on to the line like an opossum.
He caught his breath and gazed up at the aerostat, uncer-
tain whether to climb up to the balloon or down to the
ground.

Then he saw Bolo lean over the rim of the basket, his
arm cocked to hurl the boomerang in his fist, Clint could
climb down the rope faster than he could ascend it. He half
slid down the line, the harsh hemp burning his bare hands
and feet.

Bolo threw the boomerang. It whirled in a wide arch
and sizzled above Clint's head before traveling full circle
to return to the aborigine. Clint kept climbing down the
rope. He glanced up again to see Carlo raise the crossbow
to his shoulder.

Carlo aimed his weapon at the Gunsmith. Clint glimpsed down at the ground below. He had less than ten feet left to go. The Gunsmith released the rope as Carlo fired his bow. A bolt hissed past Clint, passing over his head, almost parting his hair.

Clint landed on a pile of used canvas, kept for repairs on damaged tents. He tumbled across the ground and sprawled on his back, staring up at the sinister black hull of the aerostat. The sound of footfalls rushing toward him drew his attention to a tall figure who rapidly approached.

"Clint!" Dexter Dolby called out. "Catch!"

The veterinarian threw a familiar metallic object to the Gunsmith. Clint's fingers eagerly snatched the pistol from the air. It was the Gunsmith's double-action Colt .45 revolver.

"Clever, Adams!" Feltrinelli's voice bellowed from the balloon. "But you forgot about your girl friend!"

The Gunsmith jammed his revolver into his belt and seized a large piece of canvas almost eight feet long and three feet wide. Martha screamed. Clint realized they were about to throw the girl out of the basket.

"Grab it," the Gunsmith told Dolby, swinging one end of the canvas to him. "And hold tight!"

The young man caught the canvas and nodded, aware of what the Gunsmith planned. Martha screamed again. Clint followed the sound and moved toward it. Then the girl's body suddenly plunged from the sky.

Clint and Dolby stretched out the canvas like a firemen's net and held it firmly. Martha fell into the center of the canvas, the force of her descent contributing to her weight, nearly ripping the net from the men's hands.

"Martha," Clint said as they lowered her to the ground. "Are you hurt?"

"I almost had a heart attack," she replied. "But I'm okay."

A crossbow bolt hurtled from above and struck the ground near the girl. Clint retaliated by firing two rounds at the balloon. The tether line suddenly dropped limply to the ground. Someone in the balloon had cut it to allow the craft to float away freely.

"Save your bullets," Dolby suggested. "Unless one of them presents a target, you won't hit anyone."

"And we've got problems here on earth," Martha added.

Clint turned to see two of Feltrinelli's hired gunmen rush forward with pistols in their fists. The Gunsmith's Colt snarled, pumping two bullets into the chest of the closest aggressor. The man fell as his partner leaped for cover behind a wagon.

"Where's my gunbelt?" Clint asked.

"I left it in your room," Dolby answered.

"I've only got two bullets left," the Gunsmith declared as he saw two more gunmen advance from the big top. "Give me the gun I loaned you before."

"I must have lost it on my way here," the young man replied sheepishly.

"Oh, shit," Clint muttered.

He threw himself to the ground beside Martha as a volley of gunshots erupted from the trio of enemy hootowls. Bullets spat dirt inches from his head. With only two rounds left in his Colt, Clint aimed carefully as the gunmen boldly advanced.

Then Dexter Dolby rose to one knee and pulled a narrow tin cylinder from his belt. The veterinarian seemed to ignore the enemy gunfire as he fished a Lucifer-head match from a pocket.

"Get down!" Clint shouted.

"Cover your eyes!" Dolby replied as he struck the match on a boot heel and lit a fuse at the end of the tube.

Dolby hurled the cylinder at the advancing gunmen. Clint didn't know what sort of trick his young ally had come up with, but he followed Dolby's instructions and shielded his eyes with his left hand.

An explosion of brilliant white light blasted away the darkness of night as if the noon sun had suddenly burst up from the ground. Even with his eyes covered, Clint found the glare painful. The howl of the enemy thugs revealed that they'd suffered far worse when they stared into the merciless flash.

The initial glare lasted only a second or two. A blob of fire crackled where Dolby's cylinder had landed. The three gunmen moaned in agony. Two had dropped their weapons to clamp both hands over their eyes. The third still held his pistol, but covered his eyes with his other hand. He blindly fired a round which didn't even come close to the Gunsmith and his allies.

"Try that again and you're dead!" Clint warned. "Drop your gun and raise your hands . . . *all* of you!"

The disabled gunmen obeyed.

"How'd you do it, Dex?" the Gunsmith asked his friend.

"Well, I'm a scientist, not a gunman," Dexter explained. "So I made a weapon I was familiar with from the study of chemistry. It's a magnesium flare."

"You blinded them," Martha remarked.

"Too bad we couldn't do something about those bastards in the balloon," the Gunsmith commented, gazing up at the vessel.

The Black Moon had made good its escape. Feltrinelli obviously hadn't wanted to confront the Gunsmith when

he realized Clint had a pistol. The balloon had risen higher
and sailed farther from the circus area than Clint would
have believed possible.

"We can't let them get away," Martha insisted.

"We won't," Clint assured her. "But first we'd better
take care of these guys."

They moved toward the gunmen who still had their
hands clasped over their eyes. One of the men was on his
knees, sobbing that he was blind and begging for help.

"It's only temporary," Dolby assured him. "Your
vision will clear in an hour or so."

"Okay," Clint said. "None of you fellas will need a
white cane and a tin cup, but if you don't take off your
gunbelts you'll all be wearing headstones for hats."

The trio groped at buckles and unfastened their belts.
When all three were disarmed, Clint ordered them to take
three steps backward. They followed instructions once
more.

Then the report of a rifle cracked and one of the gunmen
cried out as a bullet hit him in the lower back and severed
his spine. He crashed face-first to the ground.

"Get down!" Clint shouted.

"Jesus, don't kill us!" one of the surviving gunmen
cried.

"We're blind, damn it!" the other whimpered. "We
give up!"

"Your friends are shooting at you, you idiots," Clint
growled as he bent to scoop up a discarded gunbelt.

The Gunsmith suddenly rammed a shoulder into the
torso of the closest gunman and sent him stumbling into
the other blinded thug. Both men lost their balance and
fell. Clint scrambled to the nearest wagon where Martha
and Dolby had already fled for cover.

The unseen sniper opened fire again. A bullet screeched

past the Gunsmith's hurtling form as he dove for shelter.
Clint heard the familiar *click-clack* of a lever-action rifle
being cocked. A third sniper round struck the wagon and
splintered wood from a corner. The Gunsmith ducked low
and checked the gunbelt he'd confiscated, inspecting a
cartridge.

"Forty-four caliber." Clint sighed. "Did either of you
grab another gunbelt?"

"I did," Martha replied, passing it to Clint.

"I picked up one of the guns," Dolby explained, raising a Smith & Wesson pistol in his fist.

"Nice work, Martha." Clint smiled. "This belt has
forty-five-caliber ammunition."

"You may as well take this gun too," Dolby said. "I'm
not much good with one."

"You keep it," the Gunsmith replied as he replaced the
spent cartridges in his modified Colt double-action with
fresh shells. "I'll need somebody to keep that damn sniper
busy."

"What should I do?" Dolby asked.

"I saw a glimpse of the guy's muzzle flash. He's
positioned at the entrance to the big top," Clint explained
as he closed the loading gate of his revolver. "Fire a
couple shots in that direction to keep his attention while I
see if I can arrange a surprise for the bastard."

"I'll do my best," Dolby replied.

"Try to keep an eye on our prisoners too," the
Gunsmith added. "I don't think they'll try anything until
their eyes have recovered from that flare, but don't forget
those two are a couple of rattlesnakes. Don't assume
they're harmless."

"I understand," Dolby assured him.

"Okay." Clint took a deep breath. "Let's do it."

TWENTY-EIGHT

Dexter Dolby's hands trembled as he aimed the S&W pistol at the big top and pulled the trigger. His arms rose violently, unaccustomed to the recoil of a large caliber revolver. Dolby awkwardly thumbed back the hammer and fired again while the Gunsmith broke cover from the opposite end of the wagon.

Clint jogged to the side of the big tent, the .45 Colt in his fist. He glimpsed an orange tongue of flame that streaked from the canvas opening of the big top. The sniper was still shooting at the wagon. So far, so good.

He quickly crawled under the canvas and once again found himself behind the bleachers. Cautiously he moved among the benches, guided by the sound of the sniper's rifle as the enemy gunman worked the lever-action.

Clint Adams found his quarry. Franco, the lion tamer, was positioned by the tent opening with a Winchester saddle gun in his hand. The Gunsmith remained behind the bleachers as he approached Franco, who seemed totally unaware of Clint's presence.

Slipping under the benches, Clint surreptitiously drew closer to the lion tamer. He thrust the barrel of his Colt between the supports of the bleachers and aimed it at Franco before he barked a curt order.

"Drop the gun and raise your hands!" Clint commanded.

Franco responded by pivoting swiftly, swinging his rifle toward the Gunsmith's voice. The Colt roared before Franco could fire his weapon. Sparks erupted from the frame of his rifle as a .45-caliber slug struck metal. The force of the 230-grain bullet sent the Winchester hurtling from Franco's grasp and knocked the startled gunman backward. He lost his footing and fell.

"You've had it, fella," Clint said as he crawled out from under the bleachers. "Now . . ."

Franco still had no intention of surrendering. He scurried under another set of bleachers. Clint aimed his Colt at the retreating figure, held his fire for a moment and then drilled a bullet through the man's left thigh before he could drag the leg out of danger. Franco howled in agony, but he managed to haul the injured limb under the benches.

"You're just making this hard on yourself, fella," Clint warned him, but the Gunsmith ducked back behind the bleachers immediately after making the statement.

A pistol snarled and a bullet chipped wood from the edge of a bench in front of Clint. Franco had drawn his sidearm. Another shot screamed from a position three yards distant from the first. The lion tamer was crawling under the bleachers. He either planned to seek an escape route or a better position to try to gun Clint down . . . or both.

The Gunsmith approached carefully, his Colt held ready. He scooped up the discarded Winchester which had been rendered useless by the bullet which smashed its frame. Clint could neither see nor hear his opponent and Franco hadn't fired another shot at him. The lion tamer was clearly concentrating on putting some distance between himself and the Gunsmith.

Clint didn't have time to spend all night playing hide-and-seek with Franco. He had to find the lion tamer's position quickly and take care of him once and for all. Clint considered the fact that Franco couldn't see him either and quickly conceived a plan.

The Gunsmith hurled the broken Winchester at the top of the bleachers. It landed with a loud clatter and skidded down the column of benches, making plenty of abrasive noise in the process. A pistol shot followed and a flame of orange streaked from Franco's hiding place.

Clint bolted forward and fired three double-action rounds at his enemy's position to pin Franco down. Splinters spat up from benches as the bullets struck home. Clint hurled himself to the sawdust-laced ground and rolled into a prone position, his Colt pointing under the bleachers.

Franco stared fearfully into the gaping muzzle of Clint's six-gun. He desperately tried to swing his pistol at the Gunsmith. Clint squeezed the trigger of his Colt and shot Franco through the forehead.

The Gunsmith emerged from the big top and approached Martha and Dolby. The two surviving gunmen were still hugging the ground and rubbing their eyes. Clint ordered the pair to get to their feet while Martha rushed to his side.

"Clint," she began. "Are you all right?"

"Yeah," he replied. "Our sniper turned out to be Franco. He should have stuck to lion taming. Fella wasn't cut out to be a gunfighter. We'd better put our two prisoners under wraps and—"

"Clint," Dolby interrupted. "I think we've got another problem on its way."

The young veterinarian gestured with the S&W revolver, pointing at the sky. The blue balloon was heading back to the circus, having completed the fireworks display for the people of Logo.

"They probably heard the gunshots," Martha remarked.

"I doubt if they heard much," Clint stated. "Setting off those fireworks would probably cover up most other sounds."

"What are we going to do?" Dolby asked nervously.

"How long will it take them to reach this site?"

"Perhaps five minutes," Dolby replied. "Maybe less."

"Okay," Clint began as he bent to gather up a discarded stetson which had fallen from the head of one of the gunmen. "Let's take care of our prisoners and I'll tell you my plan."

"I hope it's good," Dolby remarked.

"Me too," Clint said. "Pick up one of those hats, Dex. You'll need it."

A few minutes later, the balloon hovered above the circus. The two men inside its basket stared down at the area. One had both fists clenched around a maneuvering vent line while the other held a Henry carbine ready. Both sighed with relief when they saw two men emerge from the big top and wave at the balloon.

"What the hell happened?" one of the outlaws in the aerostat basket called down to the ground crew. "We heard some shooting."

"That son of a bitch Adams got free somehow," a voice replied. "Got his hands on a gun and killed Franco afore we could gun the bastard down."

"Jesus," the pilot of the balloon said. "But you fellas killed Adams?"

"What do you reckon we'd do?" the voice from the ground asked sourly. "Sprinkle salt on his tail?"

"Just as long as the bastard is dead," the balloonist replied.

"Where'd the boss take off to in the other balloon?" the other man in the basket asked, laying down his carbine to toss a tow line to the men on the ground.

"I think he wanted to take his time killing the girl after what she'd done to his kid," came the reply. "Carlo was really pissed about that."

"Too bad," the assistant balloonist remarked. "Kinda hoped we'd all get a roll with her first."

"Maybe next time," the voice below chuckled.

As the ground crew towed the line, the balloon pilot eased down the deflation port line. The aerostat gradually descended. One of the men on the ground tied the tether cable to a stake in the ground.

"You know," the balloonist began, "I still wonder if this fireworks distraction was such a good idea. Settin' off all those firecrackers and Roman candles may have gotten everybody's attention, but it also woke up half the town. I wouldn't be surprised if the sheriff heads out here to see why the hell we pulled such a stunt at this hour. It's past midnight, for Crissake."

"Hell," one of the ground crewmen mused as he approached the aerostat to help anchor the basket with his weight, "it's okay if the sheriff shows up."

"What?" the confused balloonist glared at him. "What are we going to do if he finds Adams?"

"Question is," the other man replied as he slid his double-action Colt from his belt, "what are *you* going to do when you find him?"

The startled balloonist and his equally stunned assistant stared into the muzzle of Clint's pistol. The Gunsmith thumbed back the hammer. It wasn't necessary with the double-action revolver, but it accented the threat of his gun.

"Now, you fellas can either put down your weapons and climb out of that basket," Clint told them. "Or we'll just have to carry you out—feet first."

The pair got out of the basket without protest. Clint and Dexter Dolby escorted the outlaws at gunpoint to the big top. They found two of their comrades waiting inside, locked in the main cage used in the lion act.

"Reunion time, gents," Dolby declared as he removed a key ring and unlocked the cage door.

"What did you sons of bitches do to Franco?" the balloonist outlaw demanded.

"I think Franco is still dead," Clint replied. "He sure was when we took the keys from him. Now get in the cage."

The outlaws obeyed and joined their comrades behind bars. Martha Harlow joined Clint and Dolby. She handed the Gunsmith a stack of papers.

"I found these in Feltrinelli's cabin," she explained. "Most of the notes are in Italian, but I managed to read enough of it to know it's part of his plan to attack that cavalry convoy when it tries to transfer the gold."

"Great," Clint replied with a nod. "Now, if we can just get the whole thing translated—"

"Adams!" Sheriff Samuels snapped as he appeared at the mouth of the tent. "You were warned about trespassing on Mr. Feltrinelli's property . . . and what the hell do you have those fellers in a cage for?"

"It's a long story, Sheriff," the Gunsmith replied. "But I'll give you an edited version."

"What do you mean by that?" Samuels demanded.

"I mean I don't have time to tell you everything in detail right now," Clint explained.

"I'll get the balloon ready," Dolby declared as he rushed from the tent.

"Right," the Gunsmith agreed. "Martha, maybe you can explain everything to the sheriff while I get some sticks of dynamite out of the explosives shack."

"Hold on, Adams!" Samuels said crossly. "What do you think you're up to?"

"I'm going to stop a vulture before he can fly to the next state," the Gunsmith answered.

TWENTY-NINE

"You're sure you can bring this thing down safely?" the Gunsmith inquired as he glanced over the edge of the basket.

"Don't worry, Clint," Dexter Dolby replied cheerfully. "I told you I've handled aerostats before, although this is the first time I've actually piloted a hot air balloon."

Clint Adams shook his head with despair as he gazed down at the ground far below. He could only guess how high they were. It seemed as though they must be at least a mile up.

"I don't know why I let you talk me into this," he complained to Dolby.

"It was your idea, Clint," the young veterinarian reminded him.

"Then why didn't somebody talk *me* out of it?"

"But it's a wonderful idea," Martha Harlow insisted as she helped Dolby operate the maneuvering lines. "How else could we catch up with Feltrinelli?"

"If we'd all been rational," the Gunsmith muttered, "we would have simply reported the whole business to the federal marshals instead of flying after the son of a bitch like somebody out of a goddamned fairy tale."

Clint sourly recalled that the idea had indeed been his. It

169

had seemed logical enough at the time. Feltrinelli had fled in *The Black Moon*. The other balloon was available and Dolby knew how to operate one. So why not pursue the villain in the air?

Why not? The Gunsmith figured he must have been momentarily insane to consider such a scheme. Dolby wasn't as experienced with aerostats as the circus crew and that meant that they'd be at a distinct disadvantage when and if they caught up with *The Black Moon*— providing they didn't crash before they even got close to the other vessel.

The sun crept up over some distant hills as the gentle light of dawn filled the sky. Clint peered down at the grassy flatland. *Where the hell are we?* He wondered. *Lost and no closer to finding Feltrinelli than we had been before we left.*

"The hell with this, Dex," Clint declared finally. "We've been flying around looking for that black balloon for almost five hours. We don't even know if we're heading in the right direction."

"We most probably are," Dolby insisted. "The wind has been quite strong and blowing in this direction since midnight."

"But didn't you say a balloon can fly against the wind?"

"If the maneuvering vents are opened wide enough and one doesn't mind using up a good deal of gas from the bag," Dolby replied. "But I think it's unlikely Feltrinelli would do that. After all, it appeared that he just wanted to get away just as fast and as far as possible. The best way to do that would be to ride with the current of the wind."

"Well, I'd say he succeeded then." Clint sighed. "Let's find something that resembles civilization and—"

"Look there," Martha said in a tense voice.

Her finger pointed to a black skull shape in the distance.
It hovered in the sky, slowly climbing higher as two
sandbags were dropped from the ballast load. The
Gunsmith reached for the Henry carbine the outlaw balloonists had left behind.

"Can we get closer?" he asked Dolby.

"No need to," the young scientist replied. "They're
heading *toward* us."

Clint saw that his friend was right. *The Black Moon* was
advancing rapidly and still rising higher. The Gunsmith
wondered what Feltrinelli was up to. The impresario
would have no way of knowing that the blue balloon
wasn't filled with his own men.

But then Clint noticed the flash of sunlight on glass
which gleamed brightly above the rim of the black basket.
Someone in *The Black Moon* had a pocket telescope.

"They know we're manning the balloon," Clint
warned the others. "Feltrinelli must be planning to attack
us."

"That's why they're climbing higher," Dolby observed. "It's easier to fire down at a target than up at it."

"But they don't have any guns on board," Martha
stated.

"Carlo has a crossbow," Clint reminded her. "I
brought some dynamite along so we could lob it into *The
Black Moon*'s basket."

"I don't think we'd better try that when they're flying
so much higher than we are," Dolby warned.

"I realize that," Clint said dryly. "Can we get
higher?"

"We can drop some more ballast," the youth replied.
"But I still think we won't gain enough altitude. When
those guys landed the balloon before we captured them,
they released a lot of gas for the descent. We haven't

burned enough coal gas to replace it. We're simply not buoyant enough."

"Okay," Clint said grimly as he raised the rifle to his shoulder. "I guess I'll just have to punch a few holes in their basket. Sooner or later, I'm bound to hit somebody."

He aimed the Henry saddle gun at the undercarriage of the black balloon which now hovered directly above them. Clint fired three rounds into the ebony basket. The sour whine of bullets ricocheting off metal was his only reward.

"Son of a bitch," the Gunsmith whispered. "It's bulletproof!"

"They must have a steel plate installed in the bottom of the basket," Dolby stated, unable to conceal his admiration for the clever design.

"Wonderful," Clint grunted, gazing at the empty breech of the Henry. "And I just used up all our rifle ammo. Damn it! I should have checked this gun before we left. Who would have thought the owner would be dumb enough to just load three lousy cartridges in a Henry carbine?"

"Then we have to get at an angle where you can use your pistol," Martha commented.

"Or the dynamite," Dolby added.

"But what's Feltrinelli up to?" the Gunsmith wondered aloud.

The answer streaked down from the sky. A blazing projectile struck the side of their basket. Flame crackled at the woven wall of the carriage. Another fiery missile soon followed.

"The bastards are setting fire to crossbow bolts and shooting them at us," Clint realized.

"This basket is made of wicker," Dolby stated. "It'll burn like paper if we don't stop it!"

Martha reacted to the threat instantly. She seized the tow line and tossed it over the side. Then she grabbed the rim of the basket and leaped over it. Clint rushed to the hoop and looked over the edge, his heart racing, fearful that he'd see the girl's shapely, lithe body plunge to the ground below.

However, he hadn't counted on Martha's acrobatic skills. She'd caught the tow cable and dangled from it with one hand clasping the rope and her feet braced against the wall of the basket. With her free hand, Martha seized one of the crossbow bolts and yanked it from the carriage. The flaming quarrel dropped harmlessly to earth.

"Swing me over to the other one!" she called to the Gunsmith and Dolby.

"For God's sake, be careful," Clint urged as he grabbed the tow line.

The Gunsmith hauled Martha next to the second bolt. She pulled it from the basket and stamped a foot into the basket wall to crush the flames that had begun to spread there.

"Thank God," Dolby sighed with relief. "If she hadn't done that we might have burned up."

"Well," Clint mused, "if we didn't get rid of the dynamite in time we could have been blown up instead. What about—"

A third crossbow bolt struck the basket less than a foot from Martha's right elbow. The Gunsmith immediately hauled the girl up to the hoop. She caught the rim and perched her compact rump on the edge. Martha flashed a wide taunting smile up at the enraged face of Carlo who glared down at her from the black balloon overhead. Then she flashed her long shapely legs in a scissors kick which propelled her over the hoop and inside the basket.

"Hey, Carlo!" she called up to *The Black Moon*. "Killing your brother was a pleasure. He was a sack of shit too!"

"Good God," Dolby gasped. "Don't make matters worse!"

"I think they're already mad at us, Dex," Clint said, laughing. "Martha's trying to get them angry enough to get careless."

"They already are," she happily reported. "That last bolt wasn't on fire. That's why I let it be."

"You're fantastic." Clint smiled. He turned to Dolby and asked, "What if they try to set the balloon itself on fire?"

"Waste of time," Dolby assured him. "The canvas to the bag is coated with rubber. It won't burn very well. Coal gas is dense and contains little oxygen so it would smother any flame."

"Then I wonder what they'll try next?" the Gunsmith mused.

The answer appeared suddenly. A whirling disc revolved around the bottom of the black aerostat and traveled in a wide arch, gaining momentum as it approached the Gunsmith's balloon.

"Not this time, Bolo," Clint rasped, drawing his Colt.

The Gunsmith snap aimed and fired two rapid double-action rounds at the whirling boomerang. The big .45-caliber slugs shattered the wooden weapon in midair. Its broken fragments fell like a dead bird from the sky.

"It's not coming back to you this time, Bolo," Clint taunted. "Why don't you go after it?"

"They must have fired the last crossbow bolt to be reduced to using that boomerang," Martha remarked.

"What other weapons do they have left?" Dolby inquired.

"As far as I know they've only got Bolo's spear now," Clint replied. "But I wouldn't bet on it. Feltrinelli is a clever son of a bitch. I wouldn't be surprised by anything he did."

But the Gunsmith was wrong.

He was indeed surprised when Vito and Carlo suddenly swung down from *The Black Moon* at the ends of two tow lines. The acrobats hurtled toward the basket like a pair of flying demons, daggers clenched in their teeth.

Carlo landed nimbly on the hoop of the basket while his brother rocketed over the rim and dove into the Gunsmith. Clint's pistol bellowed, but the bullet only creased the acrobat's ribcage before Vito fell upon his opponent.

Before Carlo could hop down from his perch, Martha leaped to the ring that connected the load lines between the balloon and the basket. She caught the metal circle and quickly swung her body forward. Both long strong legs shot out as the girl unleashed a devastating kick that slammed both feet into her opponent's face.

Carlo's head snapped back from the force of the kick. A spray of blood spewed from his nostrils and two teeth hopped from his gaping mouth. The acrobat's feet slipped from the hoop and he toppled off his perch. Carlo Feltrinelli screamed as he plunged to the ground. His wail of horror filled the morning sky. It was abruptly terminated when Carlo crashed to earth.

Vito Feltrinelli had seized the Gunsmith's wrist with one hand and tried to twist the .45 from Clint's grasp as he attempted to stab the point of his dagger between the Gunsmith's ribs. Clint managed to grab the acrobat's wrist to prevent the lethal knife thrust.

The Gunsmith was rapidly losing the wrestling match

against his younger and stronger adversary. Vito succeeded in wrenching the pistol from Clint's hand. The Gunsmith tried to knee Vito in the groin, but the acrobat recalled what had happened when he first took on Clint and he blocked the attack with a thigh.

Clint instantly tried another tactic and butted his forehead into Vito's grinning mouth. The acrobat groaned. Clint yanked his right hand free and promptly smashed it into Vito's jaw. The blow knocked the would-be assassin backward.

Then Vito shrieked in agony.

A long leaf-shaped blade burst from the center of his chest. Bolo's primitive dark face appeared behind the acrobat. The aborigine had just swung into the basket, his spear held ready for battle. He had unintentionally skewered Vito.

With a savage snarl, Bolo slammed a bare foot into Vito's body and sent the corpse hurtling into Clint. The Gunsmith fell back against a wall of the basket as Bolo slashed the blade of his weapon at Clint's neck.

The Gunsmith's highly developed reflexes saved him from decapitation. He ducked under the whistling spear blade and drove a solid punch to Bolo's stomach. His fist hit hard muscle without effect.

Clint followed with a left jab to Bolo's chin and a right cross to the side of his jaw. The aborigine's head barely moved from the blows. The Gunsmith felt as if he was trying to punch out an oak tree.

Then Bolo lunged forward. Holding his spear like a bar, he shoved the shaft into Clint. The force sent the Gunsmith tumbling over the top of the basket—into the great empty sky beyond.

THIRTY

Clint Adams felt the sheer terror of plunging through space. The ground, hundreds of feet below, waited to smash his body to pulp. This time there was no rope tied around his waist. No tether line handy to save him from a bone shattering fall.

His hands clawed frantically at the side of the basket. Fingernails scraped the woven surface without securing a hand-hold. He continued to fall.

Then his right forearm struck something that checked his descent abruptly. His legs swung near the base of the basket as he clung to the sandbag which had saved his life.

Clint seized the ballast cord running along the bags and pulled himself higher. He looked up and saw an object jutting from the basket which resembled a feathered peg. It was the last crossbow bolt that had been fired into the aerostat. The Gunsmith grabbed it and prayed it would hold long enough for him to reach the hoop.

The bolt shifted and began to work loose under Clint's weight. He extended his other hand to the hoop. The bolt popped out of the basket as Clint caught the rim of the carriage. He braced a knee against the sandbags and hauled himself up, using the crossbow bolt in his fist as a climbing spike when needed.

Clint peered over the edge of the basket. Bolo had

cracked the shaft of his spear against the side of Dexter Dolby's skull. The veterinarian lay in a senseless heap while Bolo turned his attention to Martha Harlow.

The lovely and agile lady gymnast didn't prove to be an easy target. Bolo slashed and stabbed with his spear, but Martha nimbly hopped along the hoop of the carriage and swung back and forth on the load cables and ring, avoiding the murderous blade.

Then Bolo heard or perhaps *smelled* something which caused him to turn and face the opposite side of the basket. He spotted Clint Adams who was about to climb back inside the carriage.

Bolo screamed in primitive fury and charged forward, driving the point of his spear through the wicker wall of the carriage. Clint weaved out of the path of the lance, which narrowly missed him.

The Gunsmith quickly lunged at his assailant and swung the crossbow bolt in his fist. He thrust the tip of the quarrel under Bolo's chin. Sharp metal pierced the hollow of the aborigine's throat. Blood vomited from Bolo's open mouth as his eyes widened in disbelief.

Clint climbed into the basket while Bolo dropped his spear and clutched at the shaft of the bolt buried in his throat. The savage actually succeeded in yanking it from his flesh, which only unplugged a stream of crimson.

Bolo started to fall to his knees when Martha swung forward on the ring and slammed both feet between the aborigine's shoulder blades. Bolo staggered forward and Clint's leg swept low, kicking one of the savage's feet off the floor.

The result was Bolo plunged headfirst over the rim of the basket. The Australian hurtled six hundred feet to earth, his body literally bursting apart on impact.

"I don't think he cared for his trip," Clint remarked,

glancing down at the shattered, dismembered corpse below. "In fact, he's all broke up about it."

"My head . . ." Dexter Dolby groaned as consciousness returned. "What . . . happened?"

"We'll tell you later," Clint said. "Right now, you've got to operate this goddamn balloon."

"Clint," Martha began. "What are we going to do about Feltrinelli? We can't let him escape after all this."

"Damn right we can't," Clint replied. "He'd never stop hunting for us. We'd be looking over our shoulders the rest of our lives if we don't stop him here and now."

"But what can we do?" Dolby asked. "We're losing altitude and he's still hovering around overhead like a big black vulture."

"You once mentioned a device called a ripping cord that allows a balloon to make a quick, safe descent," Clint said.

"It's standard equipment on balloons now," Dolby replied. "But what—"

"How long will it take us to land if you pulled the ripping cord to this thing?" the Gunsmith demanded.

"About five minutes," Dolby answered. "Maybe less."

"Pull it," Clint said as he darted to the other side of the basket.

The Gunsmith grabbed one of the tow lines that still dangled from *The Black Moon*, the same ropes Vito, Carlo and Bolo had used to swoop down and attack them. He then reached into an open crate and extracted three sticks of dynamite.

"My God," Dolby gasped.

"Pull the goddamn ripping cord!" Clint snapped as he fished a match from his pocket.

He had previously inserted blasting caps and fuses and

crimped the dynamite so it would be ready if needed. The Gunsmith watched Dolby pull the cord, but he waited until he heard the ripping panel of the bag flap open to expel more gas before he struck the match.

Clint felt the balloon drop suddenly. He then held the flame to the closest dynamite fuse. Sparks hissed and the fuse began to sputter and burn.

Dolby operated the handling lines to help ease their descent. The black balloon above seemed to shrivel as they drifted farther apart. The enemy vessel assisted in this as Feltrinelli dropped more ballast for greater height.

Then the dynamite exploded.

The first stick of dynamite detonated the other two. The tremendous blast filled the sky with a brilliant blaze. The steel plate in the undercarriage of *The Black Moon* wasn't ample protection from such an explosion.

The ebony basket was torn apart by the blast. Assorted wreckage, including chunks of Feltrinelli, were scattered in all directions. Oddly, the black balloon itself didn't suffer enough damage to deflate. It continued to sail higher without the basket to burden it. To Clint, it seemed the balloon was relieved to be free of Feltrinelli's evil.

The Gunsmith certainly was.

However, the shock wave of the explosion affected Clint's aerostat as well. The blue balloon was violently tossed by the explosion. Their vessel landed awkwardly, the basket striking on a corner. Clint, Martha and Dolby tumbled out of the carriage onto the ground—bruised and breathless but uninjured.

"You blasted him," Dexter Dolby told Clint with a grin.

"Thank God," Martha said with a sigh, "it's finally over."

"Yeah," the Gunsmith said wearily. "We've got a long walk back to Logo, but I figure we've earned a rest."

"Rest." Martha nodded. "Before I go back to the farm to take care of my dairy business, I'm going to spend one full day and night in bed."

"Now, that's an idea that appeals to me too," Clint Adams said with a smile.

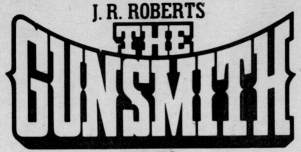

J. R. ROBERTS
THE GUNSMITH
SERIES

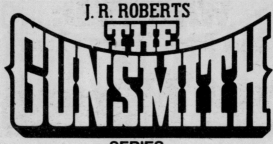

J. R. ROBERTS
THE GUNSMITH
SERIES

Prices may be slightly higher in Canada.

JAKE LOGAN

___	0-872-16823	**SLOCUM'S CODE**	$1.95
___	0-867-21071	**SLOCUM'S DEBT**	$1.95
___	0-872-16867	**SLOCUM'S FIRE**	$1.95
___	0-872-16856	**SLOCUM'S FLAG**	$1.95
___	0-867-21015	**SLOCUM'S GAMBLE**	$1.95
___	0-867-21090	**SLOCUM'S GOLD**	$1.95
___	0-872-16841	**SLOCUM'S GRAVE**	$1.95
___	0-867-21023	**SLOCUM'S HELL**	$1.95
___	0-872-16764	**SLOCUM'S RAGE**	$1.95
___	0-867-21087	**SLOCUM'S REVENGE**	$1.95
___	0-872-16927	**SLOCUM'S RUN**	$1.95
___	0-872-16936	**SLOCUM'S SLAUGHTER**	$1.95
___	0-867-21163	**SLOCUM'S WOMAN**	$1.95
___	0-872-16864	**WHITE HELL**	$1.95
___	0-425-05998-7	**SLOCUM'S DRIVE**	$2.25
___	0-425-06139-6	**THE JACKSON HOLE TROUBLE**	$2.25
___	0-425-06330-5	**NEBRASKA BURNOUT #56**	$2.25
___	0-425-06338-0	**SLOCUM AND THE CATTLE QUEEN #57**	$2.25
___	06381-X	**SLOCUM'S WOMEN #58**	$2.25
___	06532-4	**SLOCUM'S COMMAND #59**	$2.25
___	06413-1	**SLOCUM GETS EVEN #60**	$2.25
___	06744-0	**SLOCUM AND THE LOST DUTCHMAN MINE #61**	$2.50
___	06843-9	**HIGH COUNTRY HOLD UP #62**	$2.50

Prices may be slightly higher in Canada.
